Praise for *Reuniting With Strangers*

In these astonishing stories from the perspectives of migrant Filipino caregivers and their families, Austria-Bonifacio forces us to witness the emotional truths of those in servitude, and desperate to get a foot in the door.

> — CATHERINE HERNANDEZ, award-winning author
> and screenwriter of *Scarborough*

Reuniting With Strangers expertly explores the pain of migration and the bottomless hope of family. Sacrifice threads through the community—a good parent is a good provider, and a good provider is one who leaves. But when a child is abandoned over and over again, his screams are "the only sound the heart wants to make." This is the truth Austria-Bonifacio tells in language that is alive, contemporary, vivid. Read this book. You will see the world with fresh compassion.

> — KIM ECHLIN, author of *Speak, Silence*

A polyphonic chorus focusing on the lives of reunified Filipinx families, this collective of interlacing stories sings in a minor-major key of sorrow and joy, hurt and hope. Austria has invented a dazzling form of literary kundiman where all forms of love are present and invited. The result is a truly moving exploration of the psychic costs of separation, buoyed by a giant courageous heart.

> — KYO MACLEAR, author of *Unearthing*

These are stories that love you, leave you and come back to you. These stories return jagged, complicated by their departure and grown in your absence. Austria-Bonifacio documents the Filipino Canadian diaspora with the eyes of a camcorder and the heart of a Filipino surviving outside of the Philippines—holding everything.

— JANICE LOBO SAPIGAO, writer, educator and Poet Laureate Fellow with the Academy of American Poets

"Why do we call it 'the motherland' when it isn't where our mothers are?" With these words, Jennilee Austria-Bonifacio begins her extraordinary novel, inviting readers out onto the bridge that so many Filipino families navigate every day, for years, for decades, a crossing-over place of longing, confusion, anger, and complicated love. Here's the real deal, a novel that opens up the world in a new way. Be prepared for goosebumps, tears and laughter.

— KAREN CONNELLY, author of *The Change Room* and *The Lizard Cage*

REUNITING

WITH

STRANGERS

* *A NOVEL* *

JENNILEE AUSTRIA-BONIFACIO

Douglas & McIntyre

DOUGLAS AND MCINTYRE (2013) LTD.
P.O. Box 219, Madeira Park, BC, VON 2HO
www.douglas-mcintyre.com

EDITED by Caroline Skelton
COVER DESIGN by Christine Mangosing
TEXT DESIGN by Libris Simas Ferraz / Onça Publishing
PRINTED AND BOUND in Canada
PRINTED on 100% recycled paper

DOUGLAS AND MCINTYRE acknowledges the support of the Canada Council for the Arts, the Government of Canada, and the Province of British Columbia through the BC Arts Council.

CATALOGUING DATA AVAILABLE FROM LIBRARY AND ARCHIVES CANADA
Title: Reuniting with strangers : a novel / Jennilee Austria-Bonifacio.
Names: Austria-Bonifacio, Jennilee, author.
Identifiers: Canadiana (print) 20230237525 | Canadiana (ebook) 20230237533 |
    ISBN 9781771623582 (softcover) | ISBN 9781771623599 (EPUB)
Classification: LCC PS8601.U88 R48 2023 | DDC C813/.6—dc23

*For the 1200+ Filipino Talks students whose
stories kept me awake at night.*

Why do we call it "the motherland" when
it isn't where our mothers are?

Contents

CHAPTER ONE

Monolith

I CALLED HIM MONOLITH because the name sounded as strong as he looked. At thirteen pounds, he was the biggest baby that our tiny country hospital had ever seen. When he was coming out of me, I felt like he was ripping me in half. I begged for medicine to stop the pain, but when the nurses ran to the parking lot to ask my husband if he had any more money, they found that he'd spent it all on bottles of Red Horse. He said that since I was the one who got pregnant, I was the one who had to deal with it. I fell unconscious in a pool of blood.

I knew that I needed to get my son as far away from his father as possible. When Monolith stopped breastfeeding, I put him in my younger sister's care so I could leave the Philippines to work abroad. As I walked away, I heard him crying out for me, but I didn't turn back. I decided that I would only look forward to the day we reunited.

To the day when it would all be worth it.

* * *

Four years later, when my sister brought Monolith to live with me in Canada, she told me not to come to the airport.

"Ate Vera, I'll ask my friends to drive us to your place. Before Monolith comes, clean up as much as possible. If you have breakable things, put them on the highest shelves. If you have sharp things, put them inside a locked closet. And make a big plate of eggs, garlic-fried rice, and extra Spam—Spamsilog is Monolith's favourite. Ate, are you listening? Do you hear me?"

I took a day off to polish the doorknobs, mirrors, and every inch of my cracked parquet floors, and I fried enough Spam for six little boys. The entire time, my face hurt from smiling.

When they arrived at my Kerr Street apartment, I was about to scream with joy when my sister shushed me. My baby boy was sleeping in her skinny arms, and she quickly set him down on my bed.

"He's five years old and already fifty-five pounds," she said, barely looking around at my freshly cleaned apartment. Her hair was so messy that it covered most of her face, and she kept pulling her sleeves down like she was cold, though the apartment was very warm.

"You seem tired, Sora," I said. "Why don't you have a nap with him in my room? Rest ka muna—we can catch up when you're awake."

"My friends want me to stay with them until I fly back home tomorrow," she whispered, glancing at my son. "They're still outside. I don't want to keep them waiting."

I was so disappointed. I knew she had to go back to the Philippines the next day, but I wanted to stay up all night and ask her about everything I'd missed in Monolith's life. I wanted to know about his his goals, his dreams, his likes and dislikes—I longed to hear every little detail. With the twelve to thirteen-hour time difference, there was never a good time to talk to each other. If I texted her, she would only say that she'd tell me everything when she saw me in person. I had been looking forward to this moment for years.

"At least let me take you out for lunch before you leave tomorrow," I begged. "There's a Max's Restaurant in Toronto, only an hour away from here. I heard their chicken tastes almost as good as it does in the Philippines. It can be our Christmas celebration!"

Sora glanced at Monolith, her expression inscrutable. "It's too early to celebrate Christmas," she said. "I'll just text you when I get back home." She thrust an Incredible Hulk backpack into my arms, kissed his cheek, and hurried away.

She's probably tired from the journey, I thought. It was a two-hour drive from our Batangas town on the Tagaytay Ridge to the Manila airport, a fifteen-hour flight to Toronto, and a thirty-minute drive from Pearson Airport to Oakville. *Twenty hours of travel would be hard on anyone. And most of all, she's probably devastated to leave her beloved nephew behind forever. Who wouldn't be?*

I tucked Monolith under my covers and curled up next to him, breathing in his scent. He smelled like warm sun, like lush earth, like damp tropical sweat, like home. His hands were surprisingly big for his age, and I intertwined his strong fingers in mine and sighed.

I had never been happier in my life.

* * *

I woke up to him screaming.

"Calm down, Monobaby," I said in English, sleepily reaching out for my child and feeling my heart explode as he hurled himself into my open arms. But when he sank his teeth into my cheek, I instinctively yelped and shoved him away. He tumbled off the bed and fell so hard that his chin hit the floor and his mouth filled with blood.

I thought it was strange that he wasn't crying. Maybe he was too startled to notice the pain.

"Monolith, it's me, it's Mama," I said, reaching down to him. "I'm sorry I hurt you. Can you forgive me?"

He lunged at me again, his teeth grazing my other cheek. I willed myself to stay calm. I knew that he just needed to get used to me.

Monolith spotted my cellphone on the floor. He started tapping it insistently, making strange groaning noises. Since the camera had broken a long time ago, the phone was only good for making calls. I had no time for friends or social media, so I never got a new one. I never regretted this until I saw my darling son tapping at the cracked black screen in frustration.

"You remember me from my calls to your iPad, don't you? I know I didn't have any video, but you heard my voice coming from your screen, didn't you?"

He tossed the phone aside and began to wail.

He must be homesick, poor thing, I thought.

"You're not in the Philippines anymore," I said, keeping my voice soft. "You're with me now. Let me clean you up, okay? Mama loves you. I'm so happy you're in Canada. Here, do you want to see what it looks like?" I smiled earnestly and opened the curtains wide.

Pushing me aside, he stood on his tiptoes, taking in his first look of his new home in early December: the brown brick Kerr Street apartments, the overcast Oakville sky, the empty suburban sidewalks. I wished there was enough snow to make it look like a winter wonderland, but it was the kind of morning when the snow was on pause, leaving behind trees so bare that they looked dead. As Monolith surveyed his new surroundings, he didn't make a sound. I breathed a sigh of relief.

In his reflection, I saw myself. He had my expressive brown eyes, my curly black hair, and my long eyelashes, which looked so strange on a little boy. He also had his father's flat nose and big mouth, which I hoped he would grow out of someday. Just like his hands, his head was also surprisingly large for his body. But still, he had turned into such a handsome child. His skin wasn't even as dark as mine.

Look at this boy that I've made, I thought, my heart swelling with pride. "Do you know how handsome you are?" I asked, reaching out to touch his cheek.

The second my fingertip touched his skin, Monolith threw himself backwards and started to bang his head against the wall. He was cracking the cheap beige paint, but I couldn't yell at him because the only expressions I wanted to use were in Tagalog, and I promised myself that I would only speak to him in English so that he would adjust to Canadian life as fast as possible.

I bit my tongue and let him do whatever he wanted.

He'll stop, I told myself. I'd waited for so long. I'd sacrificed so much. *He'll stop eventually. Won't he?*

* * *

I tried calling Sora.

Monolith was probably acting so strangely because she'd abandoned him without properly explaining the situation. He was scared and just needed to hear her voice. I dialled her number again and again, but she wasn't answering any of my calls.

Sora had always been the selfish one, refusing to support our family by working abroad like me, claiming that her never-ending studies were too important to leave behind. She wouldn't focus on anything else but her beloved textbooks. When we were younger, I once set an egg timer beside her while she was studying and she didn't even notice when it went off. Who knew what kind of guardian she'd been? No doubt Monolith had spent years being ignored just like that ringing egg timer. My poor baby.

I tried to be patient as he tore my apartment to pieces, knocking over my snake plants, ripping apart grocery store flyers, pouring glasses of water into each other and leaving puddles everywhere.

I tried to use the sweet words that I'd heard Canadian parents say in the park: "Please make better decisions"; "I'm not disappointed in you, but in your actions"; "I need you to calm down, so would you like a time-out?" but none of those pretty Canadian admonishments ever worked.

I wanted to turn to prayer, but Monolith made it impossible. Every time I started an Our Father or a Hail Mary, he would sink his teeth into my couch cushions and start shrieking. All I could do was repeat six words from Paul's First Letter to the Corinthians: "Love is patient, love is kind; love is patient, love is kind." As I whispered the words over and over, I forced my mouth into a smile so that if Monolith turned to look at me, he would only see how much I loved him.

I thought about how my parents used to discipline me when I was young. They made me kneel on rocks, my little arms outstretched and palms turned up to the searing midday Philippine sky. I would kneel until I was shaking, until the skin on my knees cracked open and my hot blood and sweat seeped into the dirt. I would close my eyes and tell myself that the pain was good for me—that it would make me a strong woman who would be able to endure anything.

My ex-husband's parents used to discipline him by tying him to a mango tree and covering his hands in fire ants. More than once, he screamed so loudly that the town priest ran over to beg for forgiveness on his behalf. Despite the merciful intervention, my ex still turned out to be a terrible person, addicted to alcohol and prostitutes and cockfighting. It isn't Catholic to think this, but oh, I wish that priest had left him to suffer for his sins.

Whenever Monolith was ripping my couch cushions open with his teeth, throwing plastic cups across the room, or slamming himself into the bathroom door when I tried to shower, I thought of his father.

This must be my punishment for choosing a bad husband.

* * *

I had been a very skinny girl with embarrassingly dark skin. When I was a teenager, we had a series of poor harvest years, and my family couldn't afford to send me to school on the jeepney. Instead, I had to walk an hour on the dirt roads beside the unending farms of kapeng barako, with only a folded newspaper to block out the sun that burned above Mount Batulao.

But Sora was different. She was smart. With their meagre savings, my parents paid for her to study in a special science school, and rented her a room in a house beside the school gates, making it easy to keep her precious skin out of the sun. Whenever I visited her in town, I felt so ashamed that I looked more like her kasambahay than her sister.

I became so ugly that my batchmates steered clear of me, like I had a disease, like my ugliness was contagious. Even my teachers pretended that I didn't exist, always favouring the girls who could afford to whiten their skin with papaya soap. My skin was the colour of dirt, so they treated me like dirt.

When everyone else was getting ready to apply for college, I didn't know what to do. I'd worked so hard to learn English, but I knew I didn't belong at a fancy school. In desperation, I briefly considered becoming a nun, but even the priest seemed to turn his nose up at me. As my school days were ending, I felt more and more nervous about the kind of life I would lead.

But soon after my high school graduation, I went to a fiesta in the town plaza, and met the man who would change my life forever. He had ridden his motorbike over from another town, and he wore a pair of expensive-looking sunglasses, even after sunset. As

I stood against the wall alone, he looked me up and down and said the nicest thing any man had ever said to me: "You'll do." For the rest of the night, we danced beneath the waving banderitas and the glittering lights, his arms holding me so tightly that I could smell his sweet sweat. I felt blessed.

We were married a few months later. I thought it was so romantic until it was time for the Money Dance, when I realized that he wasn't holding me close because he was in love, but because he was too drunk to stand on his own. He tipped his dark sunglasses forward and focused his red eyes on mine. "If we don't dance, no one will pin money to our clothes," he said, his stinking beer breath in my face. "Make me dance."

Normally, guests would pin the money on our clothes and dance with us separately, but this was impossible. I had to ask Sora to tell our guests that we were changing the Money Dance rules.

"Just tell them that we're so in love that we can't let go of each other," I begged her. "Tell them to pin the money to our backs and go away. Please."

And as the waltz played on, I held my new husband up until my arms ached, trying to smile the entire time as our guests gave us their pesos, quietly shaking their heads.

* * *

I found a little house for us to rent. It may have been the smallest home in San Marco del Mudo, but it had cheerful yellow brick walls and a heavy wrought-iron gate that made me feel safe from the world. Every night, when he came home to me, slamming the gate so hard it woke up the neighbours, I felt at peace.

He made sure that I got pregnant immediately. At first, I thought it was sweet that he wanted to be a father. I imagined him stopping his binge drinking to stay home to play with our baby. He would turn into a young papa who would be doting, loving, perfect.

But when I was seven months pregnant, he stumbled into our room at three in the morning. "After you have this baby, you're gonna get a job abroad and you're gonna send us money," he said. "And the whole time, I'm gonna do whatever I want with whatever dirty puta I want and you won't do nothin' about it because if you do, I won't let you take the kid! That's what all good wives in this country do: they go abroad and get the hell outta their husbands' way." He stank of cheap gin and was too drunk to notice that I was crying while I pretended to sleep.

His words hurt, but in my heart, I knew he was right: I needed to go abroad, but not to support him and his many vices. I'd leave our town and work as hard as I could so that as soon as possible, I could transplant my baby and me into a better life, far away from him.

* * *

That was five years ago.

Soon after Monolith's birth, I left him with Sora. I took a contract as a caregiver for a Chinese toddler in Hong Kong, and then I left to work for a senior in Canada. After getting my Permanent Resident card, I became a personal support worker at a long-term care home in Oakville.

We are constantly understaffed, but I don't mind working double shifts; I've trained my body to sleep for only five hours a night so that I can make more money. Canadian seniors are often twice my size, so I have chronic back pain and bruises on my arms from lifting them up over and over again. But motivated by the dream of reuniting with Monolith, I became the person my parents had trained me to be: the girl who could endure anything.

As I went to the bathroom mirror and changed the bandage on my cheek, I repeated the dream that had been in my heart for years: "One day, when Monolith is a doctor, he'll take me out for my birthday dinner at Canada's fanciest restaurant. I'll tell him about our hard times and we'll laugh until our tears season our steak."

The old bandage left a sticky residue that I just couldn't rub off.

* * *

Although Monolith was loud, I noticed that he didn't communicate with words.

That useless Sora hasn't taught him English like I told her to, I thought, gritting my teeth.

Determined, I set three things in front of him: a chocolate Pocky stick, a buttery Sky Flake, and a Lay's ketchup chip. Two Filipino options and one Canadian one.

"If you want one of these, say yes," I said, my hand hovering over each snack. "Can you say yes for Mama?"

He grabbed all of them at once, cramming them into his mouth and swatting me away when I tried to brush the crumbs from his shirt.

I tried using the television. I turned on the cartoons and he froze, enthralled. Then, I turned it off. "If you want Mama to turn it on again, say yes."

He grabbed for the remote, digging his sharp nails into my arm.

"Say yes," I repeated, trying to keep calm. "Just say yes to Mama."

He sank his nails harder into my flesh.

I suddenly wondered if this was why my pretty sister, who normally loved to show off her light skin, had so desperately tried to cover her arms in front of me.

Monolith's fingernails dug in harder and harder.

"Say yes to Mama! Just say yes!" I begged, my face inches from his.

He released his grip and fell backwards onto the couch. I sighed with relief, but then he lunged forward to slap me hard across the cheek.

"MAAAAA!" Monolith shrieked. "MAAAAA!" He slapped me every time he said it.

I gasped loudly. "Monobaby! Are you saying 'Mama'?" My face stung, but my heart filled with joy. "I'm so proud of you!" I exclaimed, hugging him tightly.

For years, I'd dreamed of Monolith being in my arms and saying this one beautiful word.

In my darkest moments alone on Kerr Street, I knew that I could work as much as humanly possible, sacrificing my health and sanity, if this one golden moment came to be: my son sweetly calling me "Mama" in our new Canadian home.

Even when Monolith broke free from my arms, threw himself backwards and began to hurtle through the apartment, banging on all of the walls, I was still overjoyed.

"Paging Dr. Monolith, the smartest doctor in all of Canada!" I exclaimed, a smile on my swollen face.

*   *   *

I wanted Monolith to start school as soon as possible so that before the Christmas holidays, he could make some Canadian friends. But the night before he was supposed to start kindergarten, Monolith wouldn't sleep. For the past week, I had let him sleep anywhere, anytime. If he wanted to sleep on the couch, at the kitchen table, or even on the bathroom floor, I wouldn't move him. If he slept at four in the afternoon or at four in the morning, I didn't care. At least he was sleeping, and at least I could watch him as he rested—the only time of the day when I could admire him completely.

But on the Sunday night before school, I tried to put him to bed at eight o'clock. I managed to feed him a full meal of Spamsilog and mango juice, bathe him by wiping him down with Wet Ones, and even brush his hair without him biting my hand. He had never been so obedient before, and I was positive that when I tucked him in, he would fall asleep immediately.

Monolith, however, would not lie down. I begged him, but he launched himself off the bed and ripped my thin lace curtains down. I tried to catch him so he wouldn't get hurt, but he tumbled straight into the curtains and rolled himself up like a lumpia. When his head popped out, his thick, curly hair was covered in dust.

"Monolith, make better decisions please!" I pleaded.

He stubbornly buried his face in the folds.

"Monobaby, the curtains are dirty! Here, let Mama clean up the mess. Listen, I'm going to count to three, and you're going to unroll yourself and let Mama put you to bed. You have to get a good night's sleep so I can go to back to work at the retirement home and you can go to kindergarten tomorrow!"

He rolled himself up tighter, his head disappearing into the fabric.

"Monobaby ONE..." I began, crawling towards him. "Monobaby TWO..." I grasped the corner of the curtain and began to pull. "Monobaby THR—"

He rolled himself out and kicked me in the temple so hard that I saw stars.

Reeling backwards onto the carpet, I remembered the first time that my ex-husband made me see stars. I'd been waiting for him for hours. He'd promised to take me to the new Marian Rivera movie for my birthday. After waiting up all night, I'd fallen asleep on the couch.

"What happened to you?" I asked when I heard him clumsily trying to unlock the heavy gate. "Sweetheart, are you okay?"

Back then, my voice was sweet all of the time, even at three in the morning. It was early in our marriage and I was so innocent that I didn't know that you should never unlock a gate for an angry drunk.

"Putangina mo! Why all the questions?" he roared, slamming the gate open against the concrete wall with a bang. "You want to control me, is that it? Sige, try mo—papatayin kita! I'll kill you!" He clenched his fists and lunged at me, looking like he was possessed by a demon.

I ran past him and into our narrow street, hoping that he wouldn't hit me outside, where all of the neighbours would see.

I was wrong.

He shoved me face down onto the ground so I was at eye level with the scurrying cockroaches.

I tried to make a sound, but I was too stunned to scream or even cry.

I heard his voice in my ear. "You run outside for witnesses, but see how nobody wants to help you?" he said, delivering a swift kick to my temple.

I lifted my head in time to see the neighbours rush to close their curtains and turn off the lights.

"Does anybody care about you? No! It's because you're so ugly! So worthless! So stupid! You're nothing!"

With one more kick, I saw stars and blacked out.

For years, I was so hurt that no one did anything. Hadn't they seen me on the ground? Was it because I'd made the mistake of letting him move to their peaceful little barangay? Was this the punishment they thought I deserved?

Monolith was about to kick me in the temple a second time, just like his father. But I dodged and he fell back onto the curtains. I ran out of the room and locked the door behind me.

He howled, slamming his shoulder against the door again and again.

"Monobaby, try not to hurt yourself," I said through clenched teeth, pushing my back against the door. "Mama loves you! Say yes if you know that Mama loves you!"

The cheap wooden door started to splinter against my back. It wasn't supposed to be like this. It wasn't supposed to be this hard. We were supposed to be so happy together. Was I a bad mother if I wanted to protect him, but I wanted to protect myself, too?

I burst into tears, feeling the same hopelessness I'd felt in my darkened barrio street. But this time, I wouldn't let it happen again. This time, I would make someone help me. Pulling out my phone, I called the only person I could trust in Canada: Magda, my Polish superintendent.

"Vera? Hello? Are you crying?"

"Ma'am Magda, I'm so sorry for the late call, but it's an emergency—my son, he's locked in my bedroom and—"

"Do you need a spare key?"

"Ma'am, I'm not afraid that he can't get out," I replied, sobbing. "I'm afraid of what will happen *when* he gets out."

The superintendent paused. "Vera, are you in danger? Do you need me to bring Jan?"

I didn't hesitate to reply.

* * *

Magda came to my apartment with her husband. I'd seen him dutifully helping her around the building, carrying heavy boxes of trash and removing sickly trees from the front yard. Jan was a huge, red-haired man with a deep, booming voice that amplified in the empty hallways, making him sound commanding even when he was just making conversation about the jammed elevator door.

I'd noticed that he sometimes had red scratches across his thick arms and dark bruises on his legs, and every so often, he had a sprained finger or some swelling that made his cheek even redder than it already was. Whatever his work was during the day, I knew that it would make him ready to face the storm inside of my son.

When they showed up at the apartment, the superintendent surveyed my wrecked home, my ripped couch and dented walls, while her husband looked at me with pity when he saw the bandages and angry red marks across my face. I was so grateful that they had come to help me that I fell to my knees and cried.

Since I couldn't leave Monolith with a babysitter and I couldn't let my retirement home managers see me looking like this, I hadn't left the house in days. And after Sora had abandoned us, I hadn't spoken to anyone but Monolith and God. I had barely eaten or slept or bathed. I had been consumed with love and joy and guilt and pain, so much pain.

"Jan, go get your bag," Magda said, crouching down to me on the floor. Putting her warm hand on my back, she let me weep into her lap.

"My love, are you sure Vera wants me to do that?" he asked her, caution across his face. "I'm going to need her consent for what I'm about to do."

"Do whatever you can," I sobbed. "Whatever it is, just help me, please, I'm begging you."

He returned with a big gym bag slung across his wide shoulders. They unlocked the bedroom and quickly shut the battered door behind them.

"Hey buddy!" I heard him say in his big, friendly voice.

I plugged my ears, loudly whispering, "Love is patient, love is kind, love is patient, love is kind" to block out the sounds of Monolith's ear-splitting shrieks.

When they came out of the room, my son was in Jan's arms, red-faced and strapped into a heavy straitjacket. His arms and legs were restrained, and he made a whimpering sound like a mewling kitten. I felt sorry for him and relieved at the same time.

"Vera, I've calmed him down, but I don't feel good about it," Jan said, his grey eyes serious. "Sometimes, I take care of my sister's kid. He's a big teenager who needs a protective helmet and noise-cancelling headphones, and this is what she has me do for him, because it's the only thing that works. But I shouldn't be doing this to a little kid. You're going to have to find some professional help. My nephew has had a ton of experts assess him to figure out what he needs. Every kid's different. There are a few red flags and..."

I nodded and pretended to listen to his words about social workers and evaluations and behavioural experts and something about a spectrum, but all the while, I couldn't help thinking, *What will happen when they leave me alone? I can't help this child by myself!*

"You know, my nephew used to go to a centre nearby—it's pretty basic, but it could work," Jan said.

"You think she has money for that?" Magda snapped. "Better he goes to kindergarten, where it's free."

"Better he gets help instead of going in and getting kicked out," Jan replied.

Magda shrugged.

"Look, Vera, I could probably get you a discount if you let Monolith be in their fundraising videos..." Jan said, his voice trailing off as I turned my tear-stained face to them.

"How long will he be like this?" I asked, my voice cracking.

"You'll both be fine," Magda replied. "Look, he's calmed down now."

Jan undid the straitjacket and set my son on the couch beside me. I braced myself for the worst, but Monolith had been completely drained of his manic energy as he lay there, his eyes drowsy and his arms relaxed.

"It's a miracle," I whispered, unable to take my eyes off my transformed son. I was so exhausted that I slipped back into

Tagalog, whispering, "Salamat po, salamat po, salamat po," thanking them over and over again.

I barely noticed when they left. I watched Monolith nod off to sleep, his beautiful head lightly resting against my torn couch cushions.

I put a blanket on the parquet floor beside him, and together, we slept soundly for the first time since we reunited.

The next night, I called Jan and Magda again.

And the next night.

And the next.

I was going to become the mother that my son deserved. If getting Jan and Magda to help put him to bed at night was the secret to bringing him one step closer to going to kindergarten and therefore one step closer to becoming the famous doctor he was destined to become someday, I was willing to put up with their protests of "This is the last time we're coming" and "This is an inappropriate use of superintendent services" and "We really shouldn't be doing this anymore—we're serious this time, Vera!"

I turned a deaf ear to everything Magda and Jan said. Every night, after my baby nodded off to sleep, I told them, "Thank you for helping me. See you tomorrow!" and closed the door against their tired protests. They were my only friends in Canada, and they were the best friends I'd ever had.

After so many years apart, I was still learning how to be a good mother, and my baby deserved all the help he could get. It didn't matter what that help looked like.

Every time the straitjacket came off and he finally calmed down, I stroked his cheek and whispered three magical words in his ear: "Goodnight, Dr. Monolith."

CHAPTER TWO

The Caregiver's Instruction Manual

Section 1: Arrival

YOUR FIRST REACTION WILL BE to hug her at the airport. To show your gratitude, this is okay, but know that this is the last time that you can do it because she is not a hugger. Always remember that Canadians are polite, but they lack the warmth of Filipinos. Just like their country in mid-December, they are completely frozen on the inside.

She will hand you a gift bag with a new sweater, thick pants, thermal socks, heavy boots, a wool hat, a huge scarf, a pair of gloves, and a coat that weighs more than anything you've ever owned before. All of it will be lined in fleece, and all of it will be black. Since you've never worn so much black before, you may feel like this is a bad omen for your future abroad, but try to think positively. Even if you feel like a cross between a gorilla and an astronaut when you manage to put it all on, tell her that it's perfect.

When you leave the airport, you will feel your first blast of Canadian air. It will be worse than the air-cons in a hundred movie theatres; worse than the chills you felt on vacation in the mountains of Baguio; worse than the freezing air around the ice rink at Mall of Asia. Absolutely nothing in the Philippines will have prepared you for this moment. But when she asks, "Are you cold?" you must laugh convincingly as you lightly reply, "So this is Canadian winter? Ehh, it's not so bad!"

When you get into the car, she will ask you how your flight was, and if you slept well. Even though we both know that you will have sobbed the entire time over the husband and young sons that you left behind, you must lie to her and say, "The flight was perfect! So exciting to be on an airplane!" Make sure that you sound like an eager young college girl about to embark on an adventure. When she asks you about your family, you are only allowed to say four words: "They're fine, thank you!" Give her no more details than this because she cannot feel any guilt over bringing you here.

Note: Do not call her by her name. She will insist that you do, but this is a trap. You are her employee now. She is Ma'am to you. As for the French-Canadian man she has married, you will call him Sir.

They will beg you not to address them like this, but do not budge. If you get too close, you will ruin everything.

Section 2: The Car Ride

Do NOT CRY IN THE CAR. If you feel tears coming as you look at all of the sad, grey buildings, the huge icicles dangling from roofs like spears, and the snow drifts that could bury your old house, wipe away your tears and say, "I'm just so happy to be here!" You are allowed to miss the lush greenery and bright colours and tropical sunsets and the warmth of your loving family, but don't cry in front of anyone. Remember that out of everyone they could have hired, Ma'am and Sir chose you. There was paperwork and fees and a process that was more complicated and onerous than you will ever understand, so you must always look content and grateful.

The roads will seem so empty. No street vendors tempting passersby with their snacks, no stray cats and dogs lazily napping in the sun, no colourful tricycles parked along the sidewalks, no jeepneys and motorbikes noisily weaving in and out of traffic.

As you get closer to her neighbourhood, Ma'am will get cut off by a car ahead of her and she will let out a spew of French curses that you cannot understand. She will make an exasperated comment like "Montréalers drive like maniacs!"

You must laugh politely about this, although you both know that a Montréal driver wouldn't last a day in the Philippines, where the traffic lights and lane markings are merely road art, where the motorbikes send pedestrians scattering when they take short-cuts across sidewalks, and where drivers change lanes by brazenly darting in and out of oncoming traffic, leaning on the horn the whole time.

When you finally reach the house and go inside, Ma'am will be studying your face for a reaction. Try not to gawk at the size of the place, the expensive furniture that isn't wrapped in plastic, the luxuriously high ceilings, the floors covered in the thickest carpet you have ever seen, the all-white Christmas tree meticulously decorated with clusters of white silk poinsettias, or the strange chandeliers made of clusters of exposed bulbs that must be a pain to dust.

Do not comment on the house; it will only make her feel awkward. Just say this: "Where are the children? I'd love to meet them!"

Section 3: Meeting Sir

THE CHILDREN WILL BE IN THE PLAYROOM with Sir, who will stand up to shake your hand. His fingers will be cold and clammy and he will look like a former musician who somehow stumbled into a stifling office job that ended up paying absurdly well. Before he can get a word out, Ma'am will step between you and put a hand on his chest as she says, "This is François, my husband" with a strange, protective look in her eyes.

Note: This means that Ma'am thinks you are prettier in person than she expected. Respect her wishes and do not make eye contact with Sir, even though, with his ill-fitting plaid shirt, too-skinny jeans, receding hairline, bony frame, crooked teeth, sallow skin, and awkward meekness, he is definitely not your type. When you call your own handsome husband later that night, he will laugh heartily at Ma'am's paranoia, and this detail will make him very happy.

Section 4: Meeting the Children

THE PLAYROOM WILL BE BIGGER than your family's living room, dining room, and garage combined. The children will be in the farthest corner, ignoring the soft toys and fancy art supplies and wooden building blocks and doll houses and train sets just to cram onto one huge velvet beanbag and watch YouTube on TV. They will likely be listening to the same viral songs that your own boys love to play for hours on end. Hold back your tears when you notice this.

Repeat these words for the first of a million times: *I will not feel guilty for giving my children a better future.*

When you approach them, you will note how funny it is that, like many mixed children, instead of looking like their mother or father, they only look like carbon copies of one another, as if they'd created an entire ethnic group on their own. While their feet and hands and ears are alarmingly large, they have shiny chestnut-brown hair and big eyes and rosy skin that makes them look like dolls.

It may take some time for them to warm up to you, but the children are wonderful.

Gaël is the kind of three-year-old who loves everything sticky. He loves slime and kulangot and glitter glue and mud pies. He's very sweet and he loves to cuddle, but he is perpetually dirty. Always bring extra wipes for when he reaches up to hold your hand.

Ariane is the baby. It seems funny to say this, but it's true: she loves Pinays. When she meets other yayas in the street, she will play all of our games. She flutters her eyelashes perfectly when they coo, "Beautiful eyes! Show us your beautiful eyes!" and she happily squeezes her little fists and opens them again when they say, "Close open, close open! Close open, close open!" The funniest thing, though, is that when they say, "Where's the light?" she will point at a streetlamp and then, because it makes you kiss her every time, she will point at you. She is only fourteen months old, but you have already taught her what the last name "Liwanag" means. To her, you are light.

Geneviève is four years old, and she loves to eat. But while she will obediently finish a bowl of defrosted local blueberries, she craves tropical flavours, like pineapple, bananas, and, most of all, mangoes. This a major problem for Ma'am, who constantly reminds them, "Children, we're on the 100-mile diet! That means if it wasn't grown within 100 miles, then we don't eat it!" It will break your heart that Geneviève's tastebuds long for the flavours of a country that she will never be taken to. Mix a bit of sugar into her sad, sour little blueberries when Ma'am isn't looking.

Note: Ma'am will get upset because Geneviève's name doesn't sound nice in your Tagalog accent—"Jon-Bee-Ebb." This is why it's better not to call Geneviève anything.

If you are wondering what the children call their parents, you will be relieved to know that they call their father "Papa"—the same in French and Tagalog. But they call their mother "Maman." Don't pronounce the "n" like you would in Tagalog—let it echo a little in the back of your mouth and come forward, a soft French letter that chases all of the other letters away.

Ask the children to call you "Yaya." It may seem strange at first, but it's good to create this boundary early on. If Ma'am protests, just tell her that this is how children address their nannies back home, so it doesn't feel strange to you.

"But you're not just a nanny to us!" Ma'am will say.

She doesn't really mean that.

Most importantly, you should know that she is no longer Benita. Now, she is "Benoîte." She's had people call her that ever since she came to Montréal for her studies at McGill, where she met Sir in the dorms on the first day and his roommate remarked that Benita was the name of the building's cleaning lady who looked exactly like her; was it her mother?

When she breezily tells you that Benoîte means "blessed" in French, ignore the spirits of all of your ancestors rising inside of you in unison as they shout, "Benita meant 'blessed' in Latin first! Puuutanginang batang to! Should've just kept the name!"

Bite your tongue if you have to. Bite it until you draw Liwanag blood.

Section 5: Language

It has taken me a long time to come to this realization, but you and I have to pity Ma'am.

Before I explain to you about using Tagalog in the house, you have to understand where she is coming from. She grew up in a rural Québécois town called Bedford in the 1970s, at a time when there were no Filipinos in books or on television, no Filipino songs on the radio, no Filipinos in politics or in the movies. There was no one for her to look up to.

Her parents worked as home-care nurses, struggling so much as they mastered French that they never spoke Tagalog to her. They didn't introduce her to any Filipino children because there weren't any. They sent her to schools where she wasn't just the only Filipino, but she was the only student with black hair.

Ma'am wasn't like us. She didn't grow up learning about national heroes like José Rizal, Andrés Bonifacio, or Gabriela Silang. She didn't know about Gloria Diaz being the first Pinay to win Miss Universe, or Maria Ylagan Orosa bringing her banana ketchup from Batangas to the world, or Dado Banatao and his amazing journey from Cagayan Valley farm boy to Silicon Valley billionaire. Nobody told her anything. For her, the Philippines wasn't a place to admire, to honour, to respect.

It was just the place that her parents left behind.

So try to be empathetic towards Ma'am when she asks you not to speak Tagalog to the children.

Since they are learning French and English, she'll say they might get confused—but as you know, back home, children learn Filipino and English, and some even go to special schools to learn Mandarin or Korean or German. A child's mind is elastic and capable of so much, but Ma'am doesn't see it like that.

When you get frustrated, remember that Ma'am and Sir are already being kind because they aren't making you learn French. So in return, even the smallest Tagalog words are off-limits.

- Instead of "Aray!" say "Ouchie!"
- Instead of "Hayyy!" say "Oopsie!"
- Instead of "Huwag!" say "Please don't do that!"

And above all, remember that Ma'am doesn't want them to learn "po" and "opo." No "May I have this, po?" or "Can I play downstairs, po?" or even "Opo, Maman."

"But it's a sign of respect to their elders," you'll say. You'll think that you're already making it easier by not asking the children to learn how to use "ho" like Batangueños, but she won't see it that way.

"Those words are so old-fashioned. We don't use them in Canada," she'll snap back.

It's not that she thinks that the kids shouldn't learn about the Philippines. If there's been an earthquake, a volcanic eruption, or a typhoon, Ma'am will point it out when it shows up on the news. "Kids, look at what's happening in the Philippines!" she'll say, pointing to the horrific images flashing on TV. "See, not everyone is fortunate enough to live in Montréal."

When the disaster is especially bad, Ma'am will look at you with concern and ask if you know anyone affected. Even if you actually do, you must always say no. Why?

Because then Ma'am will want to make them a balikbayan box (note that she'll insist on calling it a "Care Package") and she'll fill it with the most useless things: old plates that are one chip away from shattering, baby onesies with food stains on the front, old puzzles with missing pieces, and children's toys that need batteries but she won't send batteries. She'll send black plastic containers and plastic cutlery that she collected from take-out meals, overpowering perfume-scented candles that she was planning on regifting anyway, a few pairs of stilettos with broken heels, and a bunch of tarnished necklaces that get all tangled up together in a reused Ziploc bag. When she mails all of this junk to your affected friend, you'll get a bewildered all-caps text in the middle of the night like *HOY! WHY DID YOU SEND ME CANADIAN GARBAGE?!?* And you'll have to say that it comes from a good place even though you're not totally sure if it does.

Section 6: Culture

MA'AM HAS RULES about story time, too.

When the kids watch the same Disney movie for the twentieth time, you'll be so bored that you'll be tempted to tap into the tales we grew up with and give them the real stories that sparked our imaginations, teaching us how to act, what to fear, and how to be proud of who we are.

But remember, this is not what Ma'am wants.

You cannot talk about the shokoy and sirena beneath the waters, but you *can* talk about Ariel. You cannot talk about the duwende and their homes in the anthills, but you *can* talk about the Seven

Dwarves. You cannot talk about the magical diwata, but you *can* talk about Tinker Bell.

Every time the children beg to watch *Frozen* for the millionth time, try to steer them towards *Moana*, because between the Polynesian coconut islands, the multi-generational households, and the courageous brown-skinned girl's quest to save her people, this is where you will feel most at home. And if they get tired of it and they just want to listen to music, try to choose songs by Princess Jasmine or Mulan, because at least their ears will be filled with Lea Salonga's golden Pinay voice. Remind them that these princesses transform into Filipinas when they sing, and that's the real magic of Disney.

Sometimes you'll overhear Ma'am on the phone, talking to her friends about how happy she is that you're here so that the kids can connect with their Filipino culture. But before you can teach the children the classic Filipino tales, like why the pineapple has so many eyes or why the ampalaya has such a bitter flavour, Ma'am will remind you that the children already have their favourite books.

There's the one with the bear who wears a shirt but no pants and licks honey off his paws. Then there's the one with a shrieking, manic pigeon who, for some reason, wants to drive a bus. Ma'am especially likes the one with the starving caterpillar with holes in his fruits that look like gunshot wounds. Ma'am loves to buy them books, but only if the main character is an animal.

You can read these until your eyes bleed, but don't try to tell the children the stories that we grew up with. Because Ma'am didn't grow up with them, they mean nothing to her.

Except for that one story.

It has been her favourite ever since I told it to her when we first met, back when she was a little girl visiting the Philippines. It was a story passed down by our great-grandmother as a cautionary tale.

Do you know the one about how the Filipino got a flat nose?

Once upon a time, there was a great boat that came to shore. The Maker was aboard, and he summoned all of the people in the world to come and pick up their noses. Everyone was so excited as they came forward to choose the loveliest noses that perfectly fit their faces.

But the Filipino was nowhere to be seen! He was being lazy, always saying that he would leave in a minute, but then having a snack, playing a game, or taking another nap. Finally, as the sun began to set, he decided to go to the boat.

But everyone else was already coming back.

"My nose is so sharp!" one person bragged.

"And mine is so narrow!" another boasted.

The Filipino began to run, but by the time he reached the boat, it was already pulling away from the shore.

Dejected, he sank down to the ground and began to cry when he spotted a nose in the dirt. It had been stepped on, so it was deformed and didn't look as nice as the sharp, narrow noses, but it was the best nose he could find.

He put on the nose and went back to show his friends.

"Your nose is so flat!" they chided him. "See, that's what you get for being a lazy Filipino!"

On a humid afternoon when she was too jetlagged for a siesta, I had told this ridiculous story to Ma'am to make her laugh.

Thirty years later, she still loves it so much that it'll make you sick.

She'll tap her finger on each of the children's noses and say, "See, that's why you have such perfect noses—your Papa's people arrived early, so they got the best ones!"

If he is within earshot, Sir will clear his throat awkwardly and say, "Mais non, Benoîte, that's not true, I think that the Filipinos, they have great noses!"

And Ma'am will laugh and say, "Don't be silly—that's why I got plastic surgery!"

Whenever she talks about her plastic surgery (and she will bring it up a lot because her colleagues from Lebanon and Iran have all done the same and they always tell her that her new narrow nose suits her so much better), it will be hard for you not to want to hide your own nose behind your hands and cry. But remember that the Liwanags have a distinctive nose, with pronounced nostrils that flare up just so. It's a flat but proud nose. So when she mentions her surgery, just say, "I'm going to check on the laundry" and leave the room.

Section 7: Laundry

You must constantly have a load of laundry going when Ma'am and Sir are home for these three reasons:

1. So that they will see that you are hard-working and therefore a good investment.
2. So that you will always have a reason to exit a room.
3. So that you will have a quiet place to cry.

You're going to cry a lot, especially in the first months. I know it's hard to believe because she'll have sent you pictures ahead of time, and you'll see that Montréal is in the prettiest part of Canada, and the old streets look like a perfect Parisian postcard where nothing could ever go wrong.

But dark thoughts will start coming in the times when you're alone. When Ma'am and Sir are at work, you'll put the children down for their naps and wander around their expansive four-storey house with its high ceilings and thick carpets and huge windows and custom-made furniture and think, *Why am I the employee and not the employer? Did I do something wrong other than be born in the wrong country?*

You could have had the white husband and the mestizo children and the high-paying office job and the BMW and the luxurious winter coats that are dry-clean only and the closet full of stilettos with red soles and the perfect English and French accents that you could switch between so effortlessly, but here you are, nothing but a yaya, ripped apart from your husband and children because, despite the nagging, sinking feeling in your chest, you so badly want for them to live like Ma'am one day.

You'll pick up a framed picture of Ma'am, and even without her original nose, you will see the Liwanag lineage in her slightly singkit eyes and her wide smile. You will feel the generations of ancestors who fought to bring both of you into this world, and you'll wonder if they're looking down and scolding your parents for refusing to emigrate forty-five years ago when Ma'am's parents left.

They only visited once, you know.

When Ma'am was eight years old and she was still Benita, she arrived in San Marco del Mudo for her first and only visit to the Philippines. Ohh, how she cried! When I was leaving for high school, she buried herself into the folds of my uniform skirt and begged me not to leave because none of our titos and titas would speak English to her.

Pitying her, I faked being sick so that she could stay with me in my room. I made her squat down on the floor with me to learn how to play dampa with a pile of elastic bands; I snuck a bowl of sticky rice upstairs to teach her how to eat sakol-style with her hands; I taught her how to add "ho" and "oho" to her English sentences so that our family might stop calling her stuck-up. All day, I tried to make sure that she wouldn't be different so from the rest of us.

But after school, when that ugly girl from my class, Vera, came over to drop off my homework, Benita and Vera looked at each other like they were aliens.

"Ehh Adora, who's this?" Vera asked in Tagalog, her dark eyes going from Benita's well-made cotton dress that looked too fancy for pambahay, to her light brown skin that was fresh from a Canadian winter.

"This is my cousin," I said.

"Why are you staring at me?" little Benita demanded, eyeing Vera's flimsy shoes, her frizzy hair, and her dark skin. "Who are you?"

"Your cousin is strange," Vera said in Tagalog, ignoring her. "Why does she seem so different from us?"

"You just think she's different because she's from abroad. She only speaks English."

Benita thrust her chin out, her little Liwanag nose in the air. "Umm, excuse me? I'm not dumb—I know you're talking about me! What are you saying?"

Vera peered closer at Benita, scrutinizing her face. "Siguro," she said thoughtfully. "But it's more than that. Like she can do anything she wants, say whatever she wants. I want to be like that one day."

"You?" I asked, laughing. "You'll have to move to Canada to be like her! And even if you actually get there, you'll be too old to change."

"Oo nga," Vera said, a thoughtful smile spreading on her wide, flat face. "Then I want my future child to grow up in Canada."

Benita stamped her foot. "Hey! What are you saying about me and Canada?"

Vera touched Benita's cheek. "Lucky girl," she said in slow English.

As she left, we watched her thin figure disappear into the long path beside the coffee farms.

"I've never seen a Filipino with skin that dark," Benita said. "Why does she look like that?"

"Vera's home is far away from here, and her family is poor, so she doesn't have money for a ride," I explained. "She has to walk under the sun for a long, long time every day."

"I feel bad for her. What does she want to be when she grows up?"

I thought for a moment. "She wants to be you."

"Okay." Benita didn't seem surprised to hear this.

Looking back, that should have been a sign.

When you dust Ma'am's dresser, you'll see that she uses lots of whitening creams—not the soaps from the Pinoy grocery store, but the ones in expensive glass jars that make K-pop stars look like they glow in the dark.

She says it's so hard to be taken seriously in her office when she's the only POC—that means "Person of Colour"—so maybe that's why she dyes her hair light brown, drives her cream-coloured BMW, wears white silk blouses and white cashmere dresses, and lives in a house filled with white furniture. Maybe she's trying so hard to be like Sir and his family that she thinks if she whitewashes her looks and her home and all of her belongings and her children and their half-Filipino minds, then maybe that will finally make her more "Benoîte" than "Benita."

So yes. Do the laundry. And when you're alone and you have to spray Shout on the brownish cuffs of her expensive modal pyjamas, remember that it is called "Shout" for a reason. And when you're sure that Ma'am and Sir aren't home and the children are upstairs and sleeping soundly, let it out. All of those feelings about Ma'am hating herself and possibly passing it down to the next generation like a disease—all of the guilt about how you agreed to take care of her children while leaving your own sons behind—all of the frustration you carry because like Vera, you are chasing a Canadian dream—let it out.

You don't have to just shout. Scream if you want to.

Section 8: Food

MA'AM WILL SAY that one of the main reasons why they hired you is because you can make Filipino food. Her mother, Tita Pilar, was the clan's favourite cook when she was young, but she didn't pass a single recipe on to her Canadian daughter.

Luckily, right before she emigrated to Canada, Tita Pilar taught her brothers, who then taught you. Ma'am knows this.

Although Ma'am will want you to make Filipino food, know that this comes with limits.

For example:

- Arroz caldo is a no because she doesn't like to eat rice because white rice isn't local—but freshly steamed puto is a yes because she doesn't know that this is made with rice flour.
- Dinuguan is an absolute no because the idea of pork blood makes her feel sick—but lumpia with organic local pork is a yes, though preferably hand-rolled into the narrowest pieces possible so that it's mostly wrapper and oil.
- Pan de coco is a no because she won't eat coconut and she doesn't like the sugary filling—but warm, homemade ensaymada smothered in butter, cheese, and sugar is a definite yes—though she will loudly call it "brioche" whenever Sir and the children are within earshot.

And on the rare occasions when she is home alone with you, offer to make tinola. The simple combination of boiled chicken, ginger, garlic, onions, and spinach will make her close her eyes and say that it reminds her of dinners with her parents before they left this world.

If she needs baon for the next day and there is enough for her to bring to work, do not say this in front of Sir because she will find it embarrassing. His friends once made a joke that tinola is basically chicken-water, and it has stuck in her head ever since. Do not remark that the gravy that they slather on their poutine is made with chicken broth, and is therefore, technically, also chicken-water.

They take poutine very seriously here. She won't think that's funny.

Section 9: Outings

MA'AM SAYS THAT she wants the children to have an appreciation for the food they eat, so she will want you to take them grocery shopping at least twice a week.

Remember, this is not like going to the San Marco palengke and picking up fruits and vegetables from Mang Aday, casually exchanging the latest juicy tsismis about who secretly emigrated in the middle of the night and who would divorce if divorce was legal in the Philippines and whose good-for-nothing younger siblings are failing their exams.

In Montréal, Ma'am wants you to go to shops where the locals will never talk to you.

Québec Biologique is just around the corner. They have free delivery, but Ma'am won't let you consider this because she wants you to bring the children there for "fresh air and life skills." This will mean that you have to force them to go even when it's windy, raining, or even—and it likely will be—snowing.

When you enter the store with three cold, cranky children who don't understand why they have to be dragged through a December snowstorm to buy Greek yogurt and peanut butter energy balls and free-run, free-range, Omega-3 eggs from the Eastern Townships for the second time that week, you will start to crumble because you don't want these Québécois shopkeepers to see you so haggard, so tired, so kawawa, again and again.

It's so humiliating that they won't look directly at you when they ring in your purchases. You're shorter than they are, so even when you're at the cash register, handing over Ma'am's card, they only make eye contact with the customer behind you as they talk and laugh above your head in a language that you will never understand.

The children know that you hate that store. That you think Greek yogurt is too thick and sour and that you think that energy balls are just a waste of money for mashed-up oats and peanut butter with someone else's fingerprints on them and that you will never understand why twelve Eastern Township eggs cost more than two of San Marco's prized chickens.

Try not to crumble when Geneviève spots the sad, stale dried mangoes in the bulk bin at Québec Biologique that taste like fibrous, sugared cardboard, and asks if you have more of the soft, fresh ones hidden in your room, the ones in bags that say "Philippine Brand" in bright red and yellow letters. She'll promise to finish it before Ma'am comes home; she just wants to lick off the sugar and then roll up each long mango onto her fingertips so that they're pointy like nails before slowly savouring each piece, one by one. You both know that Filipino dried mangoes are the best in the world, but Québec Biologique will never, ever sell them. You brought a stash in your suitcase, but she finished it. When you tell her that you don't have any left, her eyes will fill with tears.

Seeing her upset, Gaël will start to cry. He will say that he wants sapin-sapin, kutsinta, ube halaya, all of the desserts you've told him about, the stickier the better. Try to tell him no, you can't, your mama wouldn't like it, even though he will look at you with tears in his beautiful mestizo eyes and whisper that he doesn't like energy balls either and your entire heart will fill up with pride.

And of course, little Ariane will burst into tears just because she doesn't like the Québécois; they call her "chouette" and "mignonne" and while those are nice words to say to a baby, she just doesn't like the sound of them compared to the lovely familiarity of "ineng" that the other yayas use when they coo over her. When she spots her sad siblings, she conjures up that special wail that she only has for sympathetic moments like this, and your resolve to just pick up the groceries and walk back home will fade away.

Try to be strong.

I shouldn't tell you this—but just in case you need to know—for an emergency, maybe—Côte-des-Neiges has some Filipino businesses, and it's only a fifteen-minute walk away.

Ma'am knows about Pinoyville. She knows that it's down the hill, on Victoria Avenue. She'll say that she never goes there, that the food isn't within the 100-mile diet, that there are crooks lurking in the streets.

Ma'am hates Pinoyville. But her children love it.

They'll feast on fresh pancit bihon and crispy lumpia at Cuisine de Manille, happily dipping their eggrolls in the bright, sweet sauce. When they finish their meal off with creamy leche flan, they'll beg to lick the plate clean, laughing as they dip their little tongues in the sugary syrup. And most of all, they will be absolutely delighted when the servers turn up the Filipino Christmas music and attempt to teach them how to sing "Ang Pasko ay Sumapit," cheering them on every time they get a few words right.

At Isles Pinoy Depot, you can find the foods that you hide for them in your room—a container of fresh, sticky purple ube halaya for Gaël, a box of Goldilocks polvoron for Ariane, and all of the Philippine Brand dried mangoes for Geneviève that can fit in your backpack.

When you see how happy they are, you'll realize that it's a gift for them to grow up feeling at home in places like this, with the Filipino tunes blaring, and the parols casting a flashing, multicoloured capiz shell light show across their faces, and the friendly cashiers bantering with the customers in Tagalog and Bisaya and Ilokano, and the lolos and lolas who call them over just to make them practise how to mano and, of course, to tell them how cute they are when they hold out their hands and say, "Pasko po!"

The children may be mestizo, but being at home in these spaces is their birthright, you will tell yourself.

But when you get home late and Ma'am is waiting for you, know that you are in the danger zone. Because right when you're taking off the complicated, too-big black boots that she bought you, the children will do the unthinkable.

Geneviève and Gaël will eagerly go through your backpack, right there in the lobby. And Ma'am will spot them pushing the cartons of organic eggs and the Greek yogurt and the energy balls aside to get at the ube halaya and the bags of dried mangoes.

They don't know that Ma'am sees them. They haven't yet learned that mothers can see everything.

And to make it worse, Gaël will whisper in that non-whisper voice that toddlers have, "Yaya! Yaya! Can we have these now? We're hungry again!"

And Ma'am's eye will twitch.

Section 10: Discipline

MA'AM AND SIR DO NOT PUNISH the children the way we were punished. They don't pull out a wooden spoon, the rubber tsinelas, or a bamboo rod. They aren't made to kneel in front of Santo Niño for an hour, whispering their apologies, foreheads pressed to porcelain feet. They don't pull the children by their ears; they don't twist the skin on their chubby thighs; they don't make them scrub the floors; they don't threaten to take away their food—

Oh no, wait. They *do* take away their food.

"Where did you get this?" Sir will ask, plucking the ube halaya from Gaël's hands. "Is it caramel? Why is it purple?"

Gaël will burst into tears and run to you for comfort.

Meanwhile, Geneviève will clutch the dried mangoes to her chest and plead, "Papa, don't take it—it's fruit! It's not from here, but it's healthy, like blueberries! Tell them, Yaya!"

Look away as Ma'am takes the mangoes from her hands and drops them into the garbage can along with the ube and the polvoron.

"I know they're delicious, but I'm sorry, we don't eat these in our house," Sir will say, failing to comfort his sobbing children. Avoiding your eyes like he has been trained to do, he will take them to the playroom to watch *Frozen.*

Because now, Ma'am is going to discipline you.

"You know the rules—we eat local! How many times have we sent you to the grocery store with a specific list? This whole time, have you been going behind our back to buy these things? Where did you even get these? I know these aren't from Québec Biologique!"

When she sees your guilty face, she will immediately know.

"You took my children to the Filipino store? We should've known this would happen!" Yelling down to her husband, she will say, "See François, this is why we should've hired a local girl to be our au pair!"

Note: An au pair is the fancy title for educated white girls who do the exact same work that we do, but for less hours and more money and—I imagine—more respect.

She will turn to you and say, "Before he died, my father begged me to bring one of our family members over to help us with the children. 'Keep it in the family,' he said. 'Promise me. They don't have as many blessings as you do—the least you can do is bring one of your cousins to Canada!' I didn't want to do it, but what choice did I have? Say no to the wishes of a dying man?"

Sir will come back upstairs and gently pull her aside. "Alors, Benoîte, don't blame her. She is just trying to show the children their culture."

"Their culture? Their culture? But they're Québécois!"

Sir will glance at you with an apologetic expression.

This will make Ma'am even more upset.

"François, this is not like your aunt babysitting you for a few hours a month and taking you to the movies! Adora's not just their aunt—she's their yaya. And she needs to respect that—she needs to respect me! And since she won't, she can go back to where she came from!"

You will burst into tears and she will not console you. She will climb the stairs to your room and talk above your head to Sir as she announces loudly, "Adora, François and I both agree that this isn't working out," and you cannot defend yourself because you know that it's true.

This is why I recommend that you call her "Ma'am" from the beginning.

Because Ma'am will never treat you like family.

Maybe you'd expected that after the workday was over, you would go from being employer and employee to just being cousins. You would explore the city and go shopping together; you would gossip about your shared family members; she would introduce you to her friends and you would go out for long dinners with her barkada, getting tipsy off of red wine and giggling the winter nights away.

But no. There will be no adventures, no secrets, no jokes, no friendship.

I wish that someone had told me this before Ma'am brought me to Canada in the first place.

But at least I can rest easy tonight.

When you leave the Philippines to take my place tomorrow morning, you will be prepared.

Since you're a cousin-in-law instead of a first cousin like me, maybe it will be easier for you.

When I bring you to the airport, I'm going to tuck this instruction manual into your purse so that when you arrive in Canada, you will know exactly what to do.

Learn from my mistakes.

Good luck.

—Adora

P.S. Don't let the children forget how to clean themselves properly with a tabo. Ma'am doesn't need to know.

CHAPTER THREE

What's Best for the Girls

Subject: Anxious at 3 in the morning

titamama@yahoo.com.ph

To: pinayiqalummiuq@yahoo.ca

Dear Teh,

Chriselle and Gracielle are lovely thirteen-year-olds. They're responsible, beautiful, and kind. If you saw them tonight, sitting so still in church during Simbang Gabi, and then asking if they could give a generous Christmas tip to the street vendors selling fresh bibingka for Noche Buena, you'd be so proud of the young women they've become.

When they opened their Christmas gifts from you, I was so surprised that you sent them winter coats. I was worried that the twins would outgrow them before they could be worn, but then they found Canadian immigration papers tucked into the pockets. We were all shocked.

Teh, I've stayed up all night with their plane tickets in my hand. Manila- Tokyo- Vancouver- Ottawa- Iqaluit—33 hours and 3 stopovers! Will they be safe? What happens if the flight attendants are too busy to help them? What if they miss their connecting flights? What if the plane goes down? What if they're kidnapped? The girls have never travelled alone before. Anything could go wrong before they reach you. Just thinking about it makes me panic so much that I can't sleep. They're so young. Can't you send another ticket so I can travel with them?

Love,
Bunso

Re: Anxious at 3 in the morning
pinayiqalummiuq@yahoo.ca
To: titamama@yahoo.com.ph

Hi Bunso,

They'll be fine. They'll be travelling as minors, so the airport staff will help them go through security, get settled on the planes, and find their connections. I'm sorry I can't get enough time off to come get them myself, but all of my friends' kids have made the exact same journey on their own and everything worked out fine.

Bunso, you know I need to save money to support the girls when they get here, so I can't buy you a ticket. You understand, right?

So excited to finally see my girls again. Make sure they don't forget their new coats!

Merry Christmas!
Teh

Re: Re: Anxious at 3 in the morning

titamama@yahoo.com.ph

To: pinayiqalummiuq@yahoo.ca

Teh, I want to ask you something important.

Don't you remember that you never wanted them?

You didn't even mean to get pregnant—you just slept with some random guy you met at a bar on Tomas Morato before he left to become a driver in the Middle East. You were so drunk that you brought him back here. Said it was his despedida present.

When you suspected you were pregnant, I begged you not to kill the life inside of you. Remember that night in Quiapo Church? I pushed you up those narrow stairs behind the altar of the Black Nazarene, pressing your palm to the back of his foot that had been worn smooth by generations of devotees asking for help. With my hand firmly on top of yours, I told you that this pregnancy was a miracle—that it was Mama, Papa, Jesus and God's way of telling you to stop the partying, the drinking, the hookups. You cried and cried because you knew I was right.

You acted like being pregnant was a disease. Everything made you throw up—the diesel fumes on the street, the chemicals in packaged cookies, even my favourite blanket with the black swirls, which I had to keep out of your sight.

When you stopped eating, you threw up water. When you stopped drinking, you threw up air. I thought you were trying to throw up your own uterus.

And remember when you found out you were having twins? You screamed at the doctor, "Twins? I'd rather die!" I ran home to hide the knives, scissors, pills—anything you could use to hurt yourself and the girls, wrapping everything in that swirly blanket that made you sick.

You never wanted them, but I did.

Tell me you haven't forgotten.

-Bunso

Re: Re: Re: Anxious at 3 in the morning

pinayiqalummiuq@yahoo.ca

To: titamama@yahoo.com.ph

What a hurtful e-mail. Look at you, bringing up the past from what, 14 years ago?

Of course I didn't want children. But does any newly orphaned 23-year-old want kids? I was already looking after you! After Mama and Papa died, I did everything to make sure that you could live with me in Quezon City and go to UP. You were so studious because going to university was your job, but my job was to work hard so that you could do that. Sure, I blew off some steam by having fun. There was a lot going on. I needed distractions and I don't have any regrets about that.

God, you've always been so dramatic.

I'm not the same person I was back then. You should know that.

-Teh

P.S. I dare you to research "HyperemesIs Gravidarum" and "Postpartum Depression." It's more common than you think.

Re: Re: Re: Re: Anxious at 3 in the morning
titamama@yahoo.com.ph
To: pinayiqalummiuq@yahoo.ca

It's not dramatic when it's the truth. Sige, magusap tayo. Let's talk.

It's hard for me to see you as a mother when I remember how you used to be.

Your labour was easy—the girls slid into the world so quickly that it was almost like they were apologetic for having been a nuisance to you. But when we came home, you wouldn't even hold them. When they wanted to nurse, you wailed louder than your own hungry babies and pushed them away.

I sold my university textbooks for formula just to keep them alive, feeding them at all hours of the day and night while you just stayed in your darkened room. Between changing diapers and bathing them and burping them and soothing them, I completely neglected myself. When I told you that I was dizzy from lack of sleep, you were too numb to care.

My batchmates begged me to move in with them to force you to raise the girls alone, but I just couldn't. I told them that when Mama and Papa died, you took care of me, carefully budgeting our inheritance so we could stay together in Quezon City and I could go to school. I know that it wasn't easy for you.

I told them that caring for the girls was my utang na loob to you—my debt that I would repay for the rest of my life.

I don't think that way anymore. Now, you're the one with the utang na loob to me. I raised them like my own children. You're not the mother they need—you never have been.

Let them stay with me.

-Bunso

Re: Re: Re: Re: Re: Anxious at 3 in the morning
pinayiqalummiuq@yahoo.ca
To: titamama@yahoo.com.ph

Stop, Bunso. Just stop.

-Teh

Re: Re: Re: Re: Re: Re: Anxious at 3 in the morning
titamama@yahoo.com.ph
To: pinayiqalummiuq@yahoo.ca

I won't stop until I'm done.

When you received an ugly bottle of desert sand with no name, no return address, and just the words "A Remembrance of Me" etched on it, you clutched it for hours. I said it was the worst baby gift ever given in the history of fathers, but you told me that he didn't even know that the babies existed. You never wanted to try to find their father—you said that you didn't want the girls to grow up in the Middle East, or even in our little condo in Quezon City.

You wanted something more.

Before I could ask you what you meant, you went to the courtyard and smashed the bottle with a huge stone. It was like you were playing with watusi, but instead of seeing the little firecracker sparks between the rocks and laughing like we did when we were little girls, you saw the broken glass and coloured sand spill across your still-swollen bare feet and screamed.

The next day, you applied to go abroad.

Macau, France, England, Canada—after you left, you went farther and farther away and didn't come back to visit even once. And you know what else you didn't do? You didn't even ask me if I wanted to drop out of university and become a surrogate mother to your children. After all of that hard work and sacrifice, I was finally studying under the best molecular biology and biotechnology professors in the entire country! I was going to be somebody—the best education, the best network, the best career—all of it was waiting for me! But you didn't even think twice about making me drop out for the twins. Because you already knew that I would.

But twelve years later—after you worked for foreign families, received your Canadian Permanent Resident card, and got your fancy new office job—*now* you want the girls to join you in Iqaluit?

I won't allow it.

Re: Re: Re: Re: Re: Re: Re: Anxious at 3 in the morning
pinayiqalummiuq@yahoo.ca
To: titamama@yahoo.com.ph

It took me twelve years of hard work and sacrifice to get to this point. Don't make it seem like this came out of nowhere. You know that this was always the plan.

And what do you mean, you won't allow it? Who do you think you are, deciding what's best for my girls?

Subject: My Proposal
titamama@yahoo.com.ph
To: pinayiqalummiuq@yahoo.ca

Dear Teh,

Sorry it took me some time to reply. I was busy being a parent.

On the outside, Chriselle and Gracielle are identical: same height, same smiling eyes, same thick black hair.

But on the inside, the twins are so different: Chriselle is a leader and dominates her batchmates in everything from science to MAPEH to volleyball. Gracielle prefers to stay in the background, letting everyone else talk over her. Chriselle makes friends quickly and is the most popular girl in her class, but Gracielle would rather spend her time at home, reading manga and sketching landscapes in her journal. Chriselle can make anyone listen to her, but when Gracielle needs to speak up, the stress makes her sick. They couldn't be any more different.

The girls who talk to you for five minutes on your random calls are not the same girls who talk to me every single day.

With you, they sound like this: "How are you, Mama," "Thank you for the money, Mama," "We're studying hard, Mama." They're so formal, so polite. You don't know what it's like when they're having tantrums and mood swings because they want to go shopping at Uniqlo on Bonifacio High Street instead of bargaining for knock-offs at Greenhills. You don't know how hard it is to get them out of bed so that they can make it to school on time. You don't know the frustration of trying to feed them when their likes and dislikes change constantly, and that even when they're given exactly what they want, they only pick at it because they eat like birds. You don't know them like I do.

Bringing them to Nunavut is the wrong decision. I didn't finish my studies, but I remember how to research. I've pored over news articles. I've examined the maps. I've walked all over Iqaluit on Google Street View. Last night, I even studied the weather forums and saw that the temperature has only five stages: cool, cold, very cold, freezing and frigid.

Teh, there isn't even a word for "frigid" in Tagalog. How will you describe that level of cold to girls who shiver under a mall air-con?

I know that you send us so many pictures of your Filipino parties to prove that you have fun in Nunavut, but all I see is a group of lonely Pinoys eating kamayan dinners where none of the ingredients look fresh because it's all been flown in on multiple planes to get to you. You send photos each time you eat lechon, but I know it happens only once or twice a year, whereas the girls and I can feast on roasted pork anytime we want. You send us smiling pictures but they're always taken indoors because nobody goes outside. Your photos make me feel sorry for you. To be in a remote land without fresh Filipino food or the tropical sun to warm your skin? Why would you want the girls—*my girls*—to live there?

I have a proposal for you, Teh.

I want you to leave one of them behind. If you're so determined to ruin their lives, at least spare one and leave her with me.

-Bunso

Re: My Proposal
pinayiqalummiuq@yahoo.ca
To: titamama@yahoo.com.ph

You must have lost your mind.

All of my sacrifices and hardships have been for the twins.

You can't even imagine what it was like to raise other people's children abroad while missing out on my own daughters' childhoods. You think it was easy for me to leave them behind when they were still babies? I cried so much on the plane that I almost needed an oxygen mask so I wouldn't pass out.

And I never came home for a visit because I knew that if I did, I would never be able to leave them again. That's why I worked so hard for their Canadian papers—so that we could finally be together again. Forever.

Thank you for raising them. You've done a good job.

But now it's my turn.

And no, I'd never consider separating them. You claim to know what's best for them, so how could you even suggest that?

I will meet them both at the Iqaluit airport in two weeks. This is non-negotiable.

-Teh

Re: Re: My Proposal
titamama@yahoo.com.ph
To: pinayiqalummiuq@yahoo.ca

Dear Teh,

On the day you left the Philippines, after the girls waved goodbye to you, they didn't cry and scream like other babies would. Instead, they slipped their hands into mine and we ran outside of the terminal, pretending that we were airplanes. They threw themselves into my arms and we collapsed onto the ground and laughed and laughed. As your plane was taking off, they were covering my face in kisses. They understood that I was officially their mother—the way that it was meant to be.

Do you know what it's like for a nineteen-year-old girl to suddenly become a mother to two babies? To be both "Tita" and "Mama"? None of my crushes would talk to me anymore. I had to drop out of school and painstakingly balance the budgets between our inheritance and your sporadic remittances. As my friends started to date, graduate, get engaged, get married, have babies, and work, everyone looked at me with pity—like I had lost the lottery of life. But honestly, I would do it all over again.

You're lucky I was nothing like Sora—do you remember her? She went on that summer science program with me in high school. She's the one whose Ate Vera went to Hong Kong and Canada, leaving her with Monolith, that strange little boy who hated her so much that he refused to learn how to speak.

Sora was so bitter about having to look after him that she refused to quit her studies. She transferred to an online science program, but still, she couldn't keep her grades high enough because of Monolith. But then she realized that when he watched videos, he left her alone. So she bought him an iPad and let him just sit there like a zombie, rotting in front of a screen, just so she could graduate top of her class. To this day, he still doesn't say a word, and he's already five years old! I heard that she even abandoned him for an entire month just so she could have a vacation in Los Baños with her lover—her sister's drunkard husband! And after he proposed, she couldn't even look at Monolith anymore, so she dumped him in Canada and rushed back here so she could get married without any excess baggage!

See, I was never selfish like Sora. I gave everything up in order to take care of Chriselle and Gracielle. I don't only take them to school, but I make sure that they're well-rounded—we go to the zoo, Ocean Park, Star City, and every single museum in Metro Manila. The girls are my entire world, and I worked too hard for you to ruin what we have.

-Bunso

Re: Re: Re: My Proposal
pinayiqalummiuq@yahoo.ca
To: titamama@yahoo.com.ph

Dear Bunso,

I'm sorry that being a surrogate mother meant that you couldn't get your fancy UP degree, get married, or whatever else it is you wanted to do.

Get online. Now.

Chat: *PinayIqalummiuq* and *TitaMama*

PinayIqalummiuq: I'm so tired of arguing. Look, you've never had a job. Without me, you'd be broke. Stop this—or else I'll stop sending you remittances.

TitaMama: I don't care about your money! I care about the girls. I researched the school they'd go to in Iqaluit. Did you know that there's only a 39% graduation rate? You want to take them from a good private school in QC to a Canadian school where over half of their classmates will be drop-outs? Seriously?

PinayIqalummiuq: Are you seriously still arguing with me?

TitaMama: I can argue all night.

PinayIqalummiuq: Fine. I've actually met almost every teacher in Iqaluit, and they're going to watch out for the girls. They know how to support them. But look, since you've been doing all of this "research," tell me more about it since you're the expert...

TitaMama: What about climate change? I read that the ice isn't forming like it used to because it's getting warmer there. Sounds dangerous!

Pinaylqalummiuq: Aren't more super typhoons hitting the Philippines every year? Scientists predict that out of all the countries in the world, the Philippines will be impacted by climate change the most. They also predict that entire cities may end up underwater—Manila included. But I'm in danger because of climate change? You're so paranoid, it's actually funny.

TitaMama: Well, what about Seasonal Affective Disorder? The girls will only have a few hours of sunshine in the winter—it'll make them depressed! It's so cold that there aren't even sidewalks because nobody walks outside. I checked the weather and last night, it was -45. What a horrible environment!

Pinaylqalummiuq: Manila is a huge, overcrowded city with some of the worst traffic in the world. You breathe in pollution while I'm breathing clean Arctic air. True, when the girls arrive, the weather will be colder and darker than anything they've ever experienced before. But they'll have a crystal-clear sky where they can watch the northern lights dance in our own backyard. And of course I know it'll be hard for them to adapt, so I've already stocked up on Vitamin D, Vitamin C, fish oils, and SAD lamps to make them feel better. Trust me, I know how to handle Arctic life.

TitaMama: What life? There's nothing for them to do there! I toured your entire "downtown" on Google Street View. The girls are used to shopping at TriNoma, BGC, MoA. And you want them to be in a place where there isn't even a mall or a McDo?

Pinaylqalummiuq: The girls won't waste their time and money on things they don't need. And you're right—there's no McDonald's here. That just means they'll eat home-cooked meals instead of fast-food garbage. Isn't that better?

TitaMama: What about culture shock? I've seen interviews with the real locals. The girls speak beautiful English, but there, they might start to speak in that slow, weird English with an Inuit accent. And they might have to learn Inuktitut!

Pinaylqalummiuq: Wow, that's the stupidest, most racist thing you've ever said. English is English. And it'd be great if they picked up Inuktitut—the more languages they know, the better. And it's not even that hard. In Inuktitut, "tallimat" is number five—like the Tagalog "lima"! And "Tatay" is "Ataata" and "Nanay" is "Anaana." Our languages are more similar than you know. I would love it if they called me "Anaana."

TitaMama: Fine, let's talk about your insane food prices. Thirteen dollars for orange juice? Fifty dollars for a bag of sugar? Eight dollars for a papaya? What are you going to feed the girls? How are they supposed to survive?

Pinaylqalummiuq: I'm not a caregiver anymore, remember? I work at the Department of Health and Social Services. I get full benefits, a great pension, and a government salary. In two weeks, I can earn more than a Philippine government worker would make in a year! Food is expensive, but if the girls need something that's not at Northmart, I can get my orders shipped in anytime I want, or I can ask a friend to bring something back for us when they go south. Got any more questions? This is fun.

TitaMama: Crime rates in Nunavut are four times higher than the Canadian average. The girls won't be safe there.

Pinaylqalummiuq: You want to compare crime rates? Remember when we were mugged at knifepoint on the MRT? No one tried to help! Remember what the police said when we went to the station: "You're in Manila! In such a huge, overcrowded city, it's so easy to disappear." Wow. Next.

TitaMama: Iqaluit's depression rates are higher than the rest of Canada. Chriselle and Gracielle shouldn't be in a place where they'll be depressed.

Pinaylqalummiuq: Didn't I just remind you that I work for Health and Social Services? True, Nunavut has high depression rates among the locals. But there are reasons for this: the generational trauma of residential schools, the colonial destruction of their nomadic way of life, the forced relocations, the high cost of living, the broken families, and so much more. But the girls will be fine. You'll see.

TitaMama: They were born into a broken family. You take them away from me, you break their family again.

Pinaylqalummiuq: They have a loving mother, a beautiful home, and a warm, close-knit community of almost 200 Filipinos. On Saturdays, we have potlucks, and we sing karaoke and play radio bingo and mahjong. On Sundays, we go to church. And during the week, we bump into each other all over town. My friends' children will be in their school and they'll take them hiking and snowmobiling, they'll hang out at the gym and aquatic centre, they'll eat at The Snack. Everyone will look out for them. They won't just have me—they'll have an entire family.

TitaMama: The girls are all I have. Teh, don't take them away from me. Please.

Pinaylqalummiuq: You've always known that this was coming. I know that you're protective of them because you love them so much. But don't make this harder than it has to be.

TitaMama has left the chat.

Subject: What's Best for the Girls
titamama@yahoo.com.ph
To: pinayiqalummiuq@yahoo.ca

Dear Teh,

Tonight, the girls came to me with tears in their eyes. When they met up with their friends at TriNoma to tell them that they would be going to Nunavut, their friends told them stories about how their relatives went to Canada and hated it. They came home so upset. They laid their heads on my lap and I stroked their hair until we all fell asleep.

In the morning, I knew exactly what to do. I made them palabok for breakfast, topping the noodles with boiled eggs split the way they like— egg yolks for Chriselle, egg whites for Gracielle. And afterwards, we went to Ocean Park for Chriselle to visit the jellyfish that always calm her down, and then we sat for a long time at Gracielle's special spot on Manila Bay so she could paint the sunset.

Afterwards, at the end of our perfect Saturday, I took them on a special stop to Quiapo Church. I waited until the end of the day, after the crowds went home and the church was quiet. Leading them up those narrow stairs behind the altar, I had them press their hands against the smooth heel of the Black Nazarene, where I finally told them the story of how they almost weren't born at all.

You should have seen their faces.

They will never forgive you now.

So for the last time: say you'll leave them here with me.

If you don't, I'll take them to a place where you'll never find us.

You said it yourself: Manila is a huge, overcrowded city.

It's so easy to disappear.

-Bunso

Re: What's Best for the Girls
pinayiqalummiuq@yahoo.ca
To: titamama@yahoo.com.ph

Dear Bunso,

I'm sorry that I had to surprise you like that, but what else could I do? You weren't answering my calls and you wrote something that could've had you arrested. You weren't thinking clearly, so I needed to act fast.

I know you're angry at me, but let me tell you this:

I'm grateful that you were both Tita and Mama to my girls.

I'm grateful that you have always been there for me.

I'm grateful that you are my little sister, no matter what.

I'm hopeful that one day, you'll understand that I did what I had to do.

The girls are fast asleep right now. After they finally started speaking to me somewhere during the flight between Ottawa and Iqaluit, when the flight attendants went up and down the aisles to wish everyone a happy new year, I found that they are polite, responsible, and kind, just like you said they would be. I also found that they were more difficult than I expected, which you also said they would be. I told them that they can be as mad at me for as long as they like, and that I would understand.

It was hard at first, but things are slowly changing.

They've only been in school for a week, but Chriselle already loves it. She's making so many friends and winning over her teachers, and she's even made the volleyball team. Gracielle has been more content to stay in the background. But the teachers say that the other quiet girls in class, many of them Inuit, have banded together to help her get adjusted. In art class, Gracielle painted a picture of the Iqaluit sunset and showed it beside her painting from Manila Bay, and the principal hung them both up in the lobby so everyone could see how talented she is.

I'll admit that I've overheard them whispering to each other and crying at night. Sometimes, it's that they left an old sketchbook or a favourite Uniqlo shirt behind. Other times, they're upset that there are no trees here and that it's dark by mid-afternoon. I've spent so much money on art supplies and clothes, but I can't fix the weather. You were right: they hate the cold. No matter how many layers they wear, it's never enough. Whenever we're outside, they act like the wind burns their faces. But then, after they get in the car and I take them on a drive, they say that seeing all of the space and the huge skies around them makes them feel free.

They miss you so much. They say that I'm stricter and more serious than you and my palabok doesn't taste as good as yours and I keep messing up the eggs by not boiling them long enough. I'll keep trying until I finally make it right.

Tonight, the Filipino community is having a big party to welcome them, with lechon imported all the way from Ottawa. I'll send a group picture so you can see how many chosen family members the girls will have in their new lives.

Bunso, I'm sorry that I had to take the girls away from you. I can still see your panicked face; still feel your desperate hands banging against my window; still hear your frantic shrieks blending in with the girls' sobs as our taxi sped away.

But, you see, I've done you a favour. Now you can finish your studies, get your dream job, find a partner, get married. You can do anything you want, and I'll continue to send remittances for as long as you need.

That's my utang na loob promise to you for as long as I live. I owe you everything.

When you find it in your heart to forgive me, you know how to reach me. I love you so much, Bunso. We all do. I just hope that eventually, you'll agree that this is what's best for the girls.

Yours always,
Teh

CHAPTER FOUR

Seven Steps to Reuniting with Your Teenage Daughter

WELCOME TO THIS SELF-HELP GUIDE for mothers reuniting with their teenage daughters!

My name is Ginette, and as a sixteen-year-old daughter of a Filipina caregiver in Canada, I'm definitely an expert in this subject. When I was three, Ma left me in Malolos, Bulacan, and worked in Hong Kong and Taiwan before ending up in Waterloo, Ontario, where she sponsored me to be with her.

If you're wondering what to do when you finally reunite with your teenage daughter after thirteen years apart, let me show you in seven easy steps. There are multiple choice exercises in each section to test your knowledge. Don't forget to check your answers at the end!

Step One: Do Not Tell Me I'm Fat

WHEN YOU MET ME in the airport, I was about to hug you for the first time in thirteen years, but you held me at arm's length and looked me up and down. "Oh my gulay! What happened?" you exclaimed, pinching my belly. "You're so fat!"

I could have said many things back: Why did you dye your hair an unnatural shade of black? Why do your eyebrows look like they were drawn on with cheap markers? Why are your lips so wrinkled and thin?

But instead, I just looked away with tears in my eyes as you led me towards the airport exit, shaking your head in disappointment.

Please select something else that you could have said to welcome me:

a) "You're finally here! How was your flight?"

b) "I'm so happy you're here! I love you so much!"

c) "You look so grown-up now! We have so much catching up to do!"

d) "I'm so proud of you for flying across the world all by yourself!"

e) All of the above

After we got to your little house with the cupboards stocked with weird Canadian things like kale chips (chips made of salad?!?) and gluten-free cookies (what the heck is gluten?!?), I excitedly unzipped my carry-on to show you that I'd filled an entire suitcase with my favourite snack: boxes and boxes of Hello Panda.

"Look, Ma!" I exclaimed. "I brought the whole sari-sari store with me!"

You looked horrified. Zipping up my suitcase, you declared, "If I let you eat this Filipino junk, you'll get even fatter."

"I wasn't going to eat them all at once," I protested. "I didn't know if they sold Hello Panda in Canada and I—"

You shoved my suitcase into your closet. "No more snacks," you said, narrowing your eyes. I could feel you judging everything about me, from my thin black hair to my greasy brown face to my zit-covered cheeks to my soft stomach that spilled over my leggings. "Since you like this Hello Panda junk so much, you know what I'll call you? *Panda.*"

My eyes filled with tears and I wanted to argue that you could call me Ginette or Ginnie or Gin-Gin or Gigi but never-not-ever *Panda,* but before I could say anything, you pulled out your phone and video-called Mama-Lola in Bulacan.

Mama-Lola's old face filled up the screen and crinkled into a smile. "Is Gin-Gin there? How was her flight?"

I jostled for the camera. "Mama-Lola! It was so long and scary and—"

"Baby ko! How are you?"

"Ohmygosh, February in Canada is sooo cold and—"

You pushed me aside.

"What did you do to my little girl? She's so much fatter than I was at her age!"

Mama-Lola laughed, showing the gaps in her teeth. "Hay naku, Gina! You were probably malnourished from your tired yayas. Remember how all of your nannies hated you? They said you were so maarte. I remember when the last one quit, she yelled, 'That Gina is the most dramatic girl I've ever seen!'"

"I wasn't maarte—I was opinionated!"

"That's the same thing, no?"

I tried to grab the phone but you held me back.

"Mama, I can't believe you let Ginette get this fat. You spoiled her!"

Before I could tell Mama-Lola how much I missed her, you hung up the phone.

Step Two: Accept That I Have Two Mothers

I WAS USED TO THE KIND OF PARENT who always told me that I was special. Mama-Lola filled my world with a warm, unconditional love.

You were the exact opposite.

"Aren't you going to give me a house tour?" I asked, trying to lighten the mood.

"Don't fall down the stairs," you replied flatly. "You can't break any bones because you don't have your health card yet."

I thought you were joking, so I tried to hug you. "I love you too, Ma."

You backed away. "You smell like airplane. Go shower."

You went upstairs to your room and left me standing in the hallway alone. I didn't know where the shower was.

At this moment, there are so many other things you
could have said. Please pick the best one:
  a) "Thank you for the hug! I've been wanting to hug
     you for so long!"
  b) "Let me show you around so you'll feel at home."
  c) "Shower later! We have so much to talk about!"
  d) "Let's call Mama-Lola again so you can actually talk
     to her."
  e) All of the above

After you left to work abroad, Mama-Lola put your graduation picture up in our bedroom and told me that I could talk to you whenever I wanted. But since I was just a three-year-old, that didn't make any sense to me. Why would I want to talk to a piece of paper when I could just turn around and talk to Mama-Lola instead?

We shared a bed up until the morning I left for Canada.

In Waterloo, as I lay in my strange new bedroom, I missed her body next to me, the smell of freshly cooked rice on her clothes, her warm breath in my hair as she snored. I missed how she would let me wear her loose cotton dusters to bed after I had a growth spurt and none of my clothes fit me anymore. I missed the way she made me a bedtime glass of Milo mixed with filtered hot water and extra powdered milk, just the way I liked it.

I missed everything about her.

She was my mother and grandmother rolled into one: Mama and Lola.

You were just a stranger.

Step Three: Do Not Constantly Tell Me I'm Lazy

DURING OUR FIRST DAYS TOGETHER, you yelled at me all of the time. I left my clothes on the floor, my hair in the bathtub, my dishes in the sink, my bed unmade. At Mama-Lola's house, we'd always had maids to clean up after me. I never realized how messy I could be.

"Linis, linis, linis! Clean up, clean up, clean up!" you'd yell.

I tried to make my bed, but since your Canadian blankets were so unbelievably thick, I had the hardest time folding them properly. Mama-Lola only used a cotton blanket that was so thin that it was practically tissue paper—nothing compared to these huge, heavy quilts that you bought at some local Mennonite market. Maybe you forgot. But you didn't have to yell at me and say, "Even a Mennonite baby could fold this better than you!"

"I don't even know what a Mennonite is!" I cried.

I could feel myself getting sad, and so I thought of one place that could cheer me up. "Can we go to the mall?" I suggested.

You kept doing the dishes. "Too busy. Working double shifts today."

I didn't want to stay alone in your freezing, empty house. "Can I come?" I asked.

You kissed your teeth. "While I'm gone, you can clean. Clean your room, the bathroom, and the kitchen. And when you're done, do it all over again because you didn't do it right the first time."

"But I don't know how to clean," I protested.

You angrily dropped a pan into the sink, splashing cooking oil and soapy water everywhere. "I just bought you the latest iPhone, didn't I? Look it up on YouTube!"

I wanted to make you proud of me, but I was so jet-lagged that the minute you left, I fell asleep on the couch. I didn't wake up until you came home twelve hours later.

You were so mad.

"Anak ng demonyo! Ang tamad mo! Hayop ka!"

"Ma?" I asked, rubbing my eyes. "You're home already?"

"It's already eight-thirty!" you yelled, throwing your cracked imitation Louis Vuitton purse onto the floor. "You slept all day while I worked back-to-back caregiving *and* cleaning shifts so I can support you? You're so lazy! You really *are* a panda!"

"But Ma, I'm still jet-lagged and my head really hurts, and—"

"Your head hurts? You didn't do anything but sleep all day and you're complaining that your head hurts?"

There are a few things you could have said instead of yelling at me. Please select the best option:
   a) "That's true, there's a thirteen-hour time difference between Waterloo and the Philippines right now. No wonder you're jet-lagged! Here's some headache medicine."
   b) "It's been so long since we've seen each other. Let's catch up; that's more important than cleaning."
   c) "I didn't mean to yell at you. I just had a hard day at work. I'm so sorry."

    d) "When you feel better, we'll clean together and I'll
       show you how to do everything."

    e) All of the above

Ma, I really wanted to tell you about my boyfriend because I was feeling lost without him. All I could think about was how, on the day I was leaving, Janno showed up right as the driver loaded my suitcases into the van. He held my hand up until the last minute, saying, "Promise, Ginette! Promise you'll sponsor me so we can be together forever!" I sobbed so loudly that the annoyed driver yelled at Janno to go away before he ran him over.

I felt like half of my heart was missing and my entire world was falling apart.

I wished I could've talked to you about finding my one true love and feeling lost without him. But instead, you pulled me off the couch and made me scrub your bathtub with a dented box of Arm & Hammer baking soda and your dirty old toothbrush.

Step Four: Understand That Going to a New School Is Difficult

IT WAS A COLD FEBRUARY MORNING when you brought me to school for the first time. I was shaking uncontrollably, but you thought it was because it was cold.

"It's only minus eight, Panda! Don't be so maarte!" you said, propelling me up the school steps.

You didn't even realize that I was shaking because I was so nervous for the English and math assessment—the most important test I had ever taken in my life.

When it was over, the guidance counsellor told us that I would be placed in Grade 10.

My eyes welled up as I realized that I wouldn't be in Grade 11 like I was back home. "Sir, are you sure?" I asked, watching him stuff my results into an envelope as you took the package with a strange look in your eyes.

I thought you were going to stand up for me, but instead, you just left the room, storming out into the empty hallway. "All of those years of private school, and this is the best you could do?" you demanded, your brown face turning bright red. "Ang tamad mo talaga, Panda! So lazy!"

When you saw that I was about to cry, you told me that you were late for work and left me standing in the hallway.

My first class was physical education. I was stunned when I looked at my batchmates: all long hair and long legs and long arms and perfect white skin and perfect white teeth. They looked like models while I looked like the short Filipino janitor mopping up sweat outside the change room who muttered to me, "Hoy Ineng—your batchmates are six-foot Russian and Ukrainian girls. Ehh, you'll be lucky if they even let you play." I stood at the far edge of the volleyball court and tried to be invisible.

But when the ball sailed across the gymnasium and came right towards me, one of the gorgeous blondes went rushing for it with her arm outstretched. She crashed into me, scraping the floor.

"Oww, my elbow! OhmyGodwhatthehell!" Her hair was the colour of gold, and her skin was so pale it looked like she had never seen the sun. I had never been touched by someone so beautiful.

The gym teacher ran over. "Speak up when you're going for the ball!" he yelled at me. "Ya gotta call it! Say 'mine'! You can do that, can't you?"

"Sir, the new girl can't even speak English!" the blonde cried, rubbing her elbow.

I wanted to shout, "Yes I can!" but the words were frozen in my mouth. Back in Malolos, the teachers used to tell me I was good at English. But here in Waterloo, where I was already ugly and fat, suddenly, I was stupid, too.

I darted out of the gym and texted the only person I knew in this whole country:

> Ma, I don't like my new school.

I didn't have to wait long for a reply.

> Just study hard and don't be a crybaby, Panda.

I grabbed my things, threw myself through the school doors, and ran back to your house. When you finally came home, instead of asking, "How was your first day?" you saw me playing on my phone and demanded, "Why aren't you doing your homework?"

"I don't have any," I said, glad that I wasn't lying.

You snatched a slipper off of the floor and threw it in my direction, narrowly missing my thigh. "Wow Panda, you really are the most useless girl in all of Waterloo! Of course you have home-work—you just started school!"

"I promise I don't have any!" I cried.

Your face softened for a minute before it reverted back to its usual pinched state. "Then clean the bathtub again. You did a bad job earlier." You turned to tackle the pile of dishes that I had left all over the counter so that you could have the space to angrily chop a mountain of vegetables for pinakbet.

As I squatted barefoot in the tub with that soggy box of baking soda and your disgusting old toothbrush again, I thought of the text messages that you could have sent to me when I wrote, *Ma, I don't like my new school.*

Here are some options for you to pick from:
   a) I know it's hard, but just do your best. I'm proud of you for trying.
   b) Everything will get better in time. Let's talk.

c) I know change is hard. How can I make it easier
for you?

d) What happened? Give me the name of the teacher I
have to talk to.

e) All of the above

Step Five: Do Not Dismiss My Depression and Anxiety

THE NEXT MORNING, I woke up as you came into my room to put my laundry away. Wrapped up in my thick Mennonite blankets, I confessed, "Ma, I feel sad all of the time. I don't want to go to school. I miss being back home. I don't even want to get out of bed anymore. I'm depressed and I have anxiety."

You yanked the quilts away and barked two words at me: "Get dressed."

We drove and drove until we reached a strange warehouse area in the middle of nowhere. I thought we were going shopping.

But instead, you brought me to a weird basement church located below a knock-off designer furniture depot, and shoved me into a room with a big, cluttered desk. A Filipino pastor came in, groaning and clutching his lower back as he sat across from me.

Rather than leave us alone to talk, you stood behind me with your hand firmly on my shoulder like you were trying to stop me from running away. "She says she's got depression and anxiety," you blurted out, as if I'd made it up just to make you mad.

"You can't be depressed," the pastor said, shaking his finger at me. He had a patchy moustache and he wore too much gel for the few dyed black hairs left on his head. His glasses were dirty with fingerprints, and his breath smelled like patis. "Do you know how difficult it was for your mother to bring you to Waterloo? How hard she worked to satisfy the caregiver program requirements, deal with the demands of her employers, and complete all of the tests and paperwork just to bring you here?"

You stood behind me and sniffed so quietly that I couldn't tell if you were getting emotional or if you just had allergies.

"But Pastor, I'm sad. I miss home. I don't want to get out of bed."

"But you're in Canada now."

"And I'm depressed."

"But you're reunited with your mother."

"Yes, and I'm depressed."

"And you say you have anxiety, too? How did you get that?" He looked at me like I'd caught a disease.

"I think it was triggered by culture shock."

"Ha?" He looked up at you and you let out a dramatic sigh.

"Pastor, she spends all of her time on her phone. That's where she learned how to talk like this." Squeezing my thick shoulder, you added, "She won't even lose weight."

The pastor's eyes lit up as he looked me up and down. "Your weight! Yes! This is why you're stricken with these diseases. As your pastor, I recommend that you pray to our Lord Jesus Christ before each meal. Pray that you will eat less and exercise more."

"I think I need a real counsellor," I muttered.

"This will end your depression and anxiety in Jesus's name," he declared. "Amen?"

"Amen," you said together.

*   *   *

That night, you turned on your karaoke machine to sing "May Bukas Pa" on repeat. It sounded like you were trying to be a Pinay Adele, but all of your notes were flat. Maybe by singing it over and over, you were trying to tell me to have hope, that there would be a brighter tomorrow, that God would help me with my suffering—or maybe you were just practising your high notes. Either way, I didn't care. You couldn't even hear me crying because you were so damn loud. I put on the noise-cancelling headphones you'd given me and sobbed myself to sleep.

> After being told that the answer to my depression and anxiety was portion control, exercise, and Jesus, I wasn't in the mood to hear you sing. At that moment, I really needed you to talk to me. Here are some things you could have said:
>
> a) "These are some good solutions, but they're part of many things that you may need to feel better. Let's brainstorm some other strategies you might like to try."
>
> b) "What are the things that make you sad in Waterloo? What do you miss about Malolos? Let's talk about it."
>
> c) "I love you no matter what and I'm glad that you talked to me about your depression and anxiety. Tell me how I can help."
>
> d) "Let's find you a professional counsellor."
>
> e) All of the above

Step Six: Do Not Take Away My Wi-Fi

As THE DAYS WENT BY, I was spending less time talking to you and more time on my new Canadian phone. I was talking to Mama-Lola, calling her constantly so that I could feel like she was still part of my life. And after 9:30 (when you said I had to go to sleep even though it's almost impossible for any teenager to sleep at that time) I was talking to Janno.

When I called him on Valentine's Day, he kept asking when his plane ticket would be coming so we could finally be together again.

"Ginette, where is it? I keep checking my email but it's not there. What's taking so long?" Janno demanded, the hurt in his voice piercing my heart.

"I don't have any money yet," I said, my voice a whisper so you wouldn't hear. "I'm not allowed to get a job. Mama said I need to focus on school first."

I could hear Janno slamming a door and storming outside, the sounds of the Malolos morning traffic almost drowning him out. "You don't care about us! If you keep disappointing me, I'm going to cheat on you, I swear. The girls at school keep asking me if I'm single now that you're gone. You can't expect me to wait forever!"

"But I thought you loved me!"

"Love has a time limit," he said. "I can only take so much long distance. I'll tell the girls that I'm still your boyfriend, but only if you send over my sponsorship papers and my plane ticket."

"But you know I can't do that!" I cried. I dropped my phone and clamped my mouth with my hands, but it was too late.

You burst into my room and started yelling.

"You're on the phone again? It's past bedtime! See, this is why you say you're depressed and can't get out of bed—because you're staying up so late!" You grabbed my phone and I began babbling about love and heartbreak and sponsorships and money, but you couldn't understand a thing I said.

"Why do you always think you can cry and just get your way? Grow up, Panda!"

"But I'm—I'm—"

"Maldita! Bruha!" You stuffed my phone into your pocket. "I shouldn't have given you this. You'll get it back when I say you can."

"But I don't even want the phone!" I cried.

"You don't?" you sneered. "Is it because I bought you a new laptop, too? Then I'll take away your internet. When you start going to bed at a better time, I'll give you the password. Like I keep telling you, when I was your age, I went to bed at 9:30 so I could wake up at 5:30 every morning to study before school. I was a top student. When you get on this schedule, you'll get your phone and internet back. Now go to bed!"

You went to your room.

I couldn't stop crying. I knew that I had to let Janno know what you'd done, or else he would think I was ignoring him and he would cheat on me on Valentine's Day and stop loving me forever, but I was too hysterical to explain. All I could do was burst into tears and yell, "I HATE YOU, I HATE YOU, I HATE YOU!"

Honestly, I didn't mean it, but I just needed to scream. When I calmed down, I knocked on your door to apologize.

You never came out.

If you'd just opened your door, there are so many things you could have said to me. Please pick the best option:
   a) "Was there a good reason why you were on your phone past bedtime?"
   b) "Did something bad happen? Do you want to talk about it?"
   c) "Rest is important for your health. What's a reasonable time for you to turn off your phone and sleep?"
   d) "It's normal for you to miss your friends and family. It was hard for me when I first left home, too. Do you want to hear about my experience? It might help you with yours."
   e) All of the above

Step Seven: Don't Tell Me I'm Not as Perfect as You Are

WHEN YOU TAKE AWAY your daughter's phone and internet, thereby cutting off all of her ties to her old life, her depression will probably get worse.

There are many things that you should not do at this time. Which do you think is most important?

a) Do not insist on continuing to call her "Panda" to remind her that she's fat and lazy.

b) Do not point out everything she needs to clean whenever she actually works up the will to leave her bedroom.

c) Do not call her school to tell them that she's a spoiled brat and that's why she's missing classes.

d) Do not call your friends and complain so loudly that she constantly hears you say that she's a disappointment to you.

e) All of the above

When you had a day off, you finally took me out of the house. You drove to the Toronto Premium Outlets in Halton Hills. You said that we weren't going there to buy anything, and that it was just a way for me to get out of the house, but you didn't have to get mad at me every time I touched something.

"That's expensive! Put it back!"

"Mama, I'm just feeling the fabric. What's Tencel? It's so soft."

"You don't need that!"

"I didn't say I needed it. I just want to look at it."

I flipped over the price tag and we both gasped. "Things in Canada are so expensive!" we said at the exact same time, in the exact same way.

I looked at you and you looked at me.

And we both smiled the exact same smile.

Together, we blew through the Tory Burch, Burberry, and Kate Spade outlet stores, dramatically gasping and laughing as we found more and more preposterously priced things that we would never buy.

It would have been a good day.

But when I got hungry, you said that we had to go back home to eat.

"But Mama, can't we just get some pizza?" I begged. "I don't want to go home yet. There's still so many more stores. I think the cheaper ones are on the side we haven't seen yet!"

"No, we have to go home. We have leftover tempeh and kale salad, remember?"

"But Waterloo is forty-five minutes away. And Mama, I want pizza."

"What, you don't like my healthy food? You want to get diabetes? Gout? Cholesterol? Ahh, I know—you want high blood? Grabe, I knew it! You want high blood so you can die early like your Lolo and your Papa did!"

"No, I just want to stay here and—" I stopped talking as my tears began to fall.

"You're going to throw a tantrum? You want to be like that kid?" You pointed your lips at a Filipina mother being attacked by her vicious little son at the Roots outlet store. She was trying to put a sweater on him, but he kept slapping her face and screaming. With her bruised cheeks and downturned eyes, the mother looked too exhausted to react.

"He was probably raised in Canada," you said, kissing your teeth. "No manners! Walang respeto!"

"Maybe he's just trying to figure out how to make his mama listen to him," I said, watching the boy throw himself onto the floor and kick his feet against the store windows as she desperately tried to zip up a red hoodie with a Canadian flag sewn across the chest. "What if he can't talk yet?"

"No excuses for bad behaviour. He's too big to not talk. Such a brat. It's not like how it was when I was younger. We knew how to obey our elders!"

I stopped on the other side of the store windows that shuddered with every blow.

"Is that why you left me with Mama-Lola, even though she told you to stay in the Philippines with me?" I blurted out. "Didn't you disobey her when she said that you shouldn't let me grow up without a parent?"

"My Papa and my husband both died in the year you were born. I was the only one left to support you and your Mama-Lola. What was I supposed to do?"

"I don't know, maybe listen to her and not leave?"

"You don't know anything about my options at the time."

"You wouldn't know the right option even if it was written out in front of you," I snapped back.

Grabbing me by the wrist, you pulled me away from the little boy who kicked his mama away again and again, screaming like the Canadian sweater burned his skin.

And when we got home, I shut myself into my room for the rest of the afternoon to write out these seven simple steps.

I need help, Ma. And I think you need help, too.

This self-help guide is over, but I want you to know that there is actually one step that, if you'd followed it *before* any of the others, Steps 1–7 would not have been necessary at all. Now doesn't that sound nice?

Step Zero: Don't Leave Me Behind

WHEN I WAS A TODDLER and you decided to work abroad, did you know that it would be thirteen years until we saw each other again?

I built my entire life without you. I had Mama-Lola, my kasambahay, my teachers, my boyfriend. I had so many people who made me feel loved and special. I know you wish that I was different, but honestly, I wish that you were different, too.

Now that I'm here, you're constantly disappointed that I didn't turn out more like you. But how could I do that when I don't know who you are? I know that you worked hard to bring me here, to give me a nice house and a good school and the latest gadgets, but none of that means anything when I feel like you don't really hear what I have to say.

Now you've reached the end of Seven Steps to Reuniting with Your Teenage Daughter. In case you haven't figured it out already, the answer to every single exercise is e) All of the above. If you didn't circle *e* every single time, read this guide again and again until you do. When you show me that you got a perfect score, I'll be proud to announce that you're truly ready to start building a relationship with your teenage daughter who...

a) Wants to apologize and start all over again to build a better relationship with you

b) Wants to spend more time with you to get to know your past and who you are

c) Wants the internet password and her phone back please please please

d) Wants to post this online to help the millions of other Filipino parents and kids who are struggling just like us

e) All of the above

CHAPTER FIVE

Résumé of a Husband in Love

DO YOU REMEMBER THE NIGHT we married in Riyadh?

I told our friends to arrive fifteen minutes apart so that no one would know that the Filipino migrant workers were having an illegal church service inside the apartment. My housemates pulled our thick curtains shut and placed candles inside metal lanterns scavenged from a Ramadan sale, casting crescent moons and flickering stars all around the darkened room. When our undercover priest arrived, he exchanged his construction worker uniform for forbidden Catholic robes, quietly making the sign of the cross as he had someone put up a "Happy Birthday" sign on the door to ward off suspicion from our Muslim neighbours.

In my room, you unzipped a suitcase with my friend's second-hand wedding dress inside and looked at me, your face unsure.

"Darling, you'll look like an angel," I whispered, already knowing that it would fit you perfectly.

We weren't supposed to see each other before the wedding, but I just had to be near you. I was about to take you into my arms and kiss you, but you stepped back, nervously running your sweaty palms over the thin satin fabric.

"This wedding doesn't feel real," you whispered.

I opened my door a crack so you could see into the living room.

"Imagine that my apartment is a cathedral," I said, holding you close. "Do you see my noisy, rattling fridge? Imagine that it's an alcove where candles are lit beneath a statue of the Virgin Mary, whose benevolent arms are outstretched to you. And that water dispenser—imagine it's really a pane of gorgeous stained glass depicting the Holy Family. Imagine that the plastic clock on the wall is a crucifix made of solid gold; that my sticky kitchen table is an antique wooden altar; that the chipped mugs are golden chalices studded with red rubies to symbolize our everlasting love. Can you imagine it, darling? Do you see it like I do?"

You smiled shyly, blushing in the candlelight. "I do."

It was just a room of five Pinoy families sitting on the carpet, all hungrily waiting to eat Chickenjoy, bickering about whether the drumsticks were crispier from the Jollibee on Al Sulaimaniya or Al Amal. But before I walked down the aisle, I transformed our friends for you, too. Clicking on a YouTube video, I asked them to sing along with my favourite Filipino hymn, to fill the air like a choir at the Manila Cathedral. And as they dutifully sang "Tanging Yaman," they held up our phones to livestream the ceremony for our families back home so that everyone could share in our happiness.

As I took my place beside the priest, I saw your parents watching from your ancestral home in Laoag, dabbing their eyes with worn handkerchiefs, and I flashed them my happiest smile.

When you came down the aisle, your beautiful face lit by flickering lanterns, I could barely speak. And as you looked deep into my eyes and put your hands in mine, I whispered my promise to you: "This is how I will remember you for the rest of my life."

* * *

Who knew that after just one year of newlywed bliss, my employer would hire a new driver who was cheaper than me and I would lose my work contract, forcing us to be separated for the next nine years? You would follow your Arab employers as they moved their expanding family throughout the Middle East, and I would work on cruise ships that circled the globe but never docked anywhere near the deserts where you were. If I'd known that nine years would pass before you and I could live together again, I would've never let you go.

But my love for you has made these nine years fly by.

For me, it has only felt like nine days.

*   *   *

In Riyadh, you were a nanny and I was a driver for your employer's cousin. While you took care of their children, I drove my employer to his government offices, restaurants, and hotels. My entire life was spent waiting for him.

Little did you know that I was really waiting for you.

We both worked for Arab families who had all of the money in the world. We were paid better than anyone else we knew, and we had so much freedom. We could do anything, eat anywhere, travel everywhere—as long as we were married, that is. In those days, it was so difficult for single men and single women to go out in Riyadh. With separate partitions for single men in restaurants and cafés, and separate shopping times for single men at malls, and everyone always on the lookout for unmarried couples who dared to go out in public together, we both discovered that the Arab world is built for families.

Although I'd only known you for three months, we both knew that we were meant to be together. If we were actors, you and I would be the perfect Pinoy love team: Rey and his darling, destined to be cast together again and again forever. And in every single script in the long and epic storyline of our lives, we would make everyone from the writers to our millions of adoring fans weep as they witnessed our unbreakable bond.

The night I proposed to you in front of all of our friends, you and I agreed that it felt so natural to get married right away.

It was the best decision of our lives.

Even though not long after, we had to separate and I left for the first of many cruise ship contracts, you still made me the happiest man in the world when you emailed me the most incredible news: that you were pregnant with our first son.

Do you remember the package I mailed to your hospital? It was a metal statue of the Eiffel Tower to show you that even though I was far away, I would always be with you.

And it makes me smile from ear to ear to think that the one time that we reunited in Laoag, we conceived another son on our first passionate night together. I had just met my first son, and then, to be given another—it was like God and all of the saints wouldn't stop blessing our union.

Darling, we were married at twenty-eight and separated at twenty-nine. And today, nine years later, we'll finally be together again for good.

I don't care about how beautiful it is in Canada, or how peaceful it is in your chosen home of Osoyoos, British Columbia. I don't care about the way your body may have changed. I don't care about your modest house, your tedious job, or how little money you have. I only care about the one thing that matters: our eternal love.

Tonight, when we're finally alone, I'm going to take your hand in mine to reminisce. And I will ask you one question: "Do you remember the night we married in Riyadh?"

* * *

When the boys and I come to meet you in the Vancouver airport, I immediately sense that something is wrong. On a March morning, the air should be cool and damp, but British Columbia is in the middle of an unprecedented drought and heatwave.

You stiffen when I try to hug you. You turn your head when I try to kiss you. You swat my fingers away when I try to hold your hand. It's like the drought has dried up all of your affection for me.

I know that you're preoccupied with our sons, but it hurts. They've spent the last two years in Laoag, living in the little house with the view of the sand dunes, where your parents prepared them for this moment, filling them up with excitement for their new Canadian lives. From the way they jostle each other, eagerly pointing out every little thing that's strange and new, it's obvious that they will be just fine.

Although you have never driven me anywhere and it makes me uncomfortable, I let you drive us all the way to Osoyoos. As you take us down the highway, I want to play the Side A songs that we used to listen to together, but you snap at me to leave the music off. I feel like you don't want me in the passenger seat. I want you to tell me how much you missed me, how much you've been looking forward to being with me again, but you keep looking back at the boys, asking them how the flight was, if they ate, if they're hungry, if they're tired, if they're thirsty.

I have thirsted for you for all of this time, but somehow, it's like you wish I wasn't here at all.

Darling, I want you to know that during our long years apart, I have never cheated on you. Was I tempted? Of course—cruise ships are full of temptations. But while everyone around me slipped in and out of each other's cabins, becoming embroiled in intrigue, jealousy, sexually transmitted infections, and pregnancy scares, I kept my vow to you. My coworkers even nicknamed me "St. Jude" after the patron saint of lost causes because I was a lost cause to the women on every ship and in every port. I carried an old passport picture of you in my wallet, and even though my friends made fun of me because you looked so serious in it, I liked to look at it and remember how you were at twenty-eight when I would tell you a joke and your slender hands would fly up to cover your mouth when you laughed, like that laughter was a secret just for me.

In the car, I reach for your hand. When you pull away and put it to your mouth, it's a tightly clenched fist.

*   *   *

I love the little home you've made for us. You keep apologizing because it's small, but the boys don't mind the bunk beds, and I'm just glad that it's not another lonely ship cabin without you in it. The boys hug you goodnight and fall asleep immediately, but you won't stop checking on them. Are they cold? Are they hot? Do they need a snack? Some water?

I put my hand on your shoulder. "Darling, don't worry about them," I say. "They're eight and six—not babies anymore."

You push me aside, peeking into their room again. "I haven't seen Nasir and Yassir for two years," you say in a clipped voice. "I have to make up for so much lost time. I wasn't like you—going home for visits between contracts so that you're not a complete stranger to them. I was a caregiver for other families for so long. It was so hard to get all of you here. Now, I only want to take care of my boys."

"Do what you need to do," I say. "But first, let me take care of you."

You raise a patchy eyebrow and I notice the dark circles under your eyes that are, no doubt, the result of spending so many nights alone.

"Darling, for the past nine years, I've been working on ships with thousands of international passengers, going above and beyond to make them as comfortable as possible. I love taking care of people. I'm so good at it that I used to wallpaper my room in their thank-you cards. But I'm done with taking care of everyone else. Now, there's only one passenger on my ship forevermore, and that's you." I move in for a deep, long-awaited kiss, but you hold me back.

"Nasir and Yassir need school clothes and swimming lessons, and we have to pay for rent, food, utilities, gas, and more. Having all of you here is going to be expensive, and I can't do it alone. You want to take care of me? Get a job."

I try to reach out for you again, but you leave the room.

*   *   *

That night, we share the same bed, but you're so used to sleeping in the middle that you don't make space for me. You spread out like a starfish while I lie squished against the wall. As you sleep, I study every inch of you in the moonlight. A little bigger around the hips. A little saggier in the chest. A little greyer around the temples.

You pinch your mouth as you sleep, and this unsettles me. Back in Riyadh, your sleeping mouth looked like a pucker, always begging to be kissed. In the middle of the night, I would press my lips against yours again and again.

Here, you just look dissatisfied.

I try waking you up by whispering in your ear, "Darling, would you like a kiss goodnight?"

You groan and turn away.

I fall asleep dreaming of Riyadh.

*   *   *

The next morning, I see a "Help Wanted" sign in a convenience store window and eagerly introduce myself to Eun-Young, a Korean grandmother who recently arrived in Osoyoos. She is charmed by the words that I've learned over multiple shore leaves in Busan: mannaseo bangapseumnida, gamsahamnida, bulgogi, kimchi, ajumma.

"You're the most cultured person in this town," she says, and hires me on the spot.

I get paid seven dollars an hour to ring up junk food and cigarettes. After twelve hours, I come home with eighty-four dollars in cash, and I'm proud to give it all to you.

But as I hand it over, you act like the money is on fire, letting the coins and slippery Canadian bills drop to the floor.

"You're not even getting minimum wage! How will you provide for us like that?" Your dark eyes burn holes into mine as you spoon too much afritada onto the boys' plates, the potatoes spilling onto the table, staining your white tablecloth with oily tomato sauce. "Make a résumé and find a real job!"

I'm so hurt that I refuse to eat. As my food grows cold, I start to type.

Reynaldo Delmar

rey_del_mar_@yahoo.com.ph

Driver	September 30, 2008–August 2, 2010
Aman Family	Riyadh, Saudi Arabia
Cruise Ship Employee	
(Various Positions)	August 30, 2010–February 1, 2019
Holland America Line	Worldwide
Cashier	March 5, 2019–March 5, 2019
Hello Convenience	Osoyoos, British Columbia

*   *   *

The next day, as I stroll through downtown Osoyoos, my heart sinks. My cruise ships had landed in Vancouver many times before, and I naïvely thought that Osoyoos would look the same: a sparkling city of mountains and lush waterside parks, the tall green trees leading down to the shores like beachgoers eager for an afternoon swim.

Darling, I can't understand why you settled in this lonely place of parched hills and scrubby-looking trees. After years in the deserts, you chose to settle in the only desert in Canada? I always thought it was funny that I would tell you about my childhood spent catching waves on Siargao's Cloud 9 surfbreak, but you would talk about sandboarding at La Paz. Do you love it here because it reminds you of Laoag and the hot sand dunes where you used to play?

There's a lake in downtown Osoyoos, but it isn't a vibrant, deep sapphire like the ocean. It's a sad, muted grey, like a dried-up mud puddle. If this is what it looks like in March when it's supposed to be wintertime, what will this place look like in the summer?

So many closed shops, empty sidewalks, desolate streets. The only people I see are curious senior citizens who steal glances at me through closed windows. Where is everyone? Have they left because of climate change? I don't understand why you stay. Is it because you haven't toured the globe like I have?

Darling, I wish I could make you see the image of us that I would picture whenever I missed you too much. We would be standing with the boys, the open ocean behind us, sun in our faces, my arm across your shoulders as I pull you close to plant a kiss on your cheek. Happily reunited at last.

I know that dream could become a reality. I just need to find out how.

I'm about to walk back to your house when I find a man waiting at the bus stop. With his black hair, brown skin, and welcoming smile, I can instantly tell that he's Filipino.

"Kabayan!" I call out, waving my résumé. "Do you know any-one hiring?"

"Of course!" he replies, cheerfully beckoning me over. "I'm Erwan from Tarlac."

"Rey from Siargao," I reply, shaking his hand.

"Wow, the surfing capital! Tide pools and lagoons and all that nightlife, ha? Naks naman pare, so different from where you are now. Me, I used to live by a river in Tarlac that was so shallow in the dry season that even a baby could walk across it!" He laughs a little too loudly. "Anyway, my boss is always looking for new work-ers. Want me to introduce you? Pete's coming in a minute."

I nod eagerly as a truck pulls up at the bus stop and Erwan climbs in. I notice that while I'm wearing a fresh polo shirt, a crisp jacket, and pressed khakis, they're both wearing stained sweat-shirts and worn cargo pants.

Pete tips his sun-faded baseball cap as he looks me up and down. "Hey buddy, you're a little overdressed for farm work."

"Excuse me?" I ask.

He shifts his cap above his bushy eyebrows. "Hey, actually, can you speak English? Or at least, better English than those toked-out Québécois hippie kids we just hired?"

I straighten up. "I've been speaking English for my entire life, sir."

"Sir? Wow, I like that." Pete grins, showing all of his coffee-stained teeth. "Wanna be in sales?"

"Yes, that would be better for me," I reply enthusiastically. "I'm very good at marketing. On the cruise ships, I'd convince so many guests to book their next trip before they even disembarked. So many of them chose to double-dip because of me and go on a back-to-back cruise. Many of them even booked the 128-day pack-age—our longest cruise ever!"

As I try to hand him my résumé, Pete looks at me with amuse-ment and waves it away. "Just try not to smoke any weed when you're in front of customers." The words fall out of his mouth like he says them all the time.

I'm dropped off somewhere on Highway 97, at a worn fruit stand made of plywood. They unload their wares and Pete sets me up with a little plastic chair. "In the summer, we grow almost everything here: apples, apricots, nectarines, cherries, plums, pears, and peaches, too. But with this weird heatwave and drought, who knows what's gonna happen? Last year, there were snowstorms all March, but this year, the whole damn Okanagan is bone-dry. It's pretty wild. Anywho, while Erwan and I figure things out, we gotta make some money, so right now we're just selling preserves and jams."

"Jams," I echo, my mouth suddenly dry like the road.

"You don't need training to do this, eh? You got Canadian experience?"

"I worked in a local sales position up until yesterday," I say, pleased that I'm not lying.

Before I can ask him how much he'll be paying me, he gets back in the truck.

"Sell everything you can, and in a few hours, we'll be back to get you. And don't pocket any cash, okay?"

I watch the dust rise up as they drive away.

Left alone on the side of a Canadian highway, I look out at the parched hills and tumbleweeds and I think of you.

Darling, why must you make it so hard for me to take care of you?

*   *   *

When I come home, I'm covered in a layer of dust as I hand you a jar of apricot jam and a few bills and coins.

You are unimpressed.

"I told you to find a real job! What don't you understand?"

"I've had a long day," I say, wiping dirt from my face. "I'm going to take a shower."

"No you're not. You need to go outside and be with your sons."

"Why? They're fine." I open a window and call to them in the backyard. "Hey boys! Keep playing outside, okay?"

I close the window again.

You narrow your eyes at me. "The boys are crying because they were bullied. I took them to work with me and I left them to play outside with Travis and Justin, my clients' grandchildren. I was just trying to help the boys make friends before they start school, but after I went inside, they got beaten up! And why? Those horrible kids said that Nasir and Yassir sounded like terrorists because of their names. Can you believe that? This is how they treat my boys when I take care of their grandma and grandpa? It's too much!"

"So why don't we move?" I suggest gently.

"And where would we go?" you ask, your voice crisp.

I take your clammy hands in mine, warming them up with all of the love I have for you. "Darling, we can go anywhere. Over our time apart, I've seen the world. I could take you to the most beautiful places: Central Park in New York, Hagia Sophia in Istanbul, Piazza San Marco in Venice, Glacier Bay in Alaska. I could bring you anywhere you want."

Your hands go limp. "Those are places you've seen on your cruises." You spit the words out with bitterness but I don't know why.

In the backyard, the boys are still crying over their bruises.

You rush outside with ice packs, leaving me alone again.

* * *

Reynaldo Delmar
rey_del_mar_@yahoo.com.ph

Driver	September 30, 2008–August 2, 2010
Aman Family	Riyadh, Saudi Arabia
Cruise Ship Employee	
(Various Positions)	August 30, 2010–February 1, 2019
Holland America Line	Worldwide
Cashier	March 5, 2019–March 5, 2019
Hello Convenience	Osoyoos, British Columbia
Jam Seller	March 6, 2019–March 6, 2019
Highway 97 Farm	Osoyoos, British Columbia, Canada

The next day, I'm determined to find a real job. I walk to the Employment Centre and hand over my updated résumé.

I meet an employment counsellor who chews on a blueberry muffin as she speaks with an open mouth. "I see your Canadian work experience is in sales. Would you like to work in our Home Hardware Building Centre? They need a Retail Sales Associate."

I gulp. "Ma'am, if you please, I'd rather not work in sales anymore."

"Perhaps something in construction?"

"No thank you."

"Viticulture?"

"I don't know what that is."

"Wait, you're Filipino—you probably have some kind of nursing background, right? How about senior care?"

"I've noticed that Osoyoos has many seniors, and I'd like to keep it that way," I say diplomatically.

"Excuse me?"

"Not all Filipinos are meant to be caregivers," I say with a shrug. "If I worked as a caregiver, my clients would all die prematurely."

A chunk of her oily muffin falls onto my résumé. "Look, Reynaldo, you're not giving me much to work with."

I look at her computer background and notice that beneath the desktop files cluttering her screen, there is a picture of a glimmering sapphire ocean.

"Ma'am, I worked on the Holland America cruise ships for nine years. I travelled the world and served hundreds of thousands of guests. Surely that must mean something," I plead.

She perks up at this. "Osoyoos gets hundreds of thousands of visitors a year. We're a resort municipality. And now that summer seems to be coming early with this damn climate change situation, maybe I could find you something in tourism?"

My heart beats faster. "I'm very interested!" I lean forward excitedly. "Are there any tourism jobs I can do so that I'm near the water every day? And not like Osoyoos Lake, but a truly beautiful body of water?" I point my lips at her computer screen.

She thinks for a minute, chewing slowly.

"Ever heard of Kliluk—the Spotted Lake?" she asks.

*   *   *

When I come home and tell you that I found a job at Spotted Lake, you aren't happy with me. The ride is only nine minutes down the Crowsnest Highway, but there are no buses that go there, and walking from your house will take over two hours.

"I'll already have to drop Nasir and Yassir off at school, drive all over the place for my clients, pick the boys up after school, drop them off at their after-school activities, run errands, bring them home, cook dinner, clean up, and get them ready for bed. When will I find the time to chauffeur you around, too?"

"I know it'll be difficult," I say. "But that's just until I make enough money to buy us a second car."

"I need to pay off this mortgage! You seriously think that we'd use your salary for a second car?" You back away from me, your eyes burning. "I just want you to work somewhere closer. Is that too much to ask?"

"But I've tried two jobs now. Trust me, this is the only job in Osoyoos that's right for me."

"You've never even been there! Picking up garbage along the highway beside that weird lake with the holes on the surface that look like Swiss cheese—that's what they're going to ask you to do. There's no access to the actual lake, you know. No swimming, no fishing, no boating. There's no hotel, restaurant, or even a tourist information booth. It's no Lake Okanagan—nobody's renting boats so they can look for Ogopogo. It's barely a five-minute stop on the side of the road." You throw your hands in the air. "Can't you think of me just for once?"

"That's all I've thought about since the day we met!"

You step backwards, positioning yourself on the other side of the kitchen island where I can't reach out to you. "Oh that's right, the day we met and you said, 'I can't go to the malls whenever I like and I can't eat at the nicer side of the restaurants just because I'm a single man, so I'd love to be with you all of the time so I can experience Riyadh properly.'"

I shake my head. "No no, darling, that's not what I said. I said that I'd love your company as I explore Riyadh, and you agreed that it would be fun to do things together. You said that it was hard for single women too, because the Arab world was built for families. Don't you remember?"

"That wasn't an invitation for you to glue yourself to me! The next thing I knew, you were always around me, so everybody thought that we were a couple. Then, three months later, when you insisted that we get engaged and said that you'd already arranged our secret wedding, I was so young and stupid that I thought I didn't have any choice but to say yes. I can't believe I agreed to marry you in your disgusting living room!"

I feel faint. "What are you saying?"

You can't even look at me as you speak, but I get a sinking feeling that you've said all of these things to me before, in rooms where I have never been.

"After a year of being married to you, I'd had enough. I begged my employers to take me with them when they moved to Sana'a just so I could get away from you. They wanted to hire you, too, so we could stay together, but I said no—I just couldn't be near you anymore!"

I stumble backwards, clutching the thin windowsill for balance. "You moved to Yemen to get away from me? But we were just newlyweds. We were happy!"

You stand up straighter, your shoulders squared. "That's the problem with you: you only see what you want to see. You rewrite every detail like I'm just an actor in your script!"

I feel my eyes welling up, but I don't want you to see me cry. I look at my reflection in the window and wipe my eyes with my sleeve.

"While you were on your cruises, I always made sure that I was employed in deserts, never close to any port. It's not a coincidence that our entire marriage has been spent apart, Rey. I've spent the last nine years trying to stay as far away from you as possible."

I can't believe what I'm hearing, so I quickly try to remind you of better times. "But what about that one trip, when we both went back home for our anniversary? When I met your parents in Laoag and you sent them away for a week so we could have time together, just you, me and our little son? We were so happy that you became pregnant again! I've done nothing but love you and the boys since then!"

"Say our names."

"What?"

"You never say our names. Your mind is so twisted that you can't recognize that we're real people. We're just characters to you!"

"That's ridiculous! A father doesn't need to call his own family by their names. Darling, you know that!"

"Stop calling me that," you snap.

I reach to you, but you cross your arms and back away.

"Don't you remember that time we were supposed to go to Siargao together, but I was so sick that I cancelled my flight? That was all a lie—I did it so I didn't have to be near you. It's so exhausting to be around you, Rey. That's when I knew I couldn't do this—us. I hate being 'Darling.' I want you to see me for who I really am, but I don't think you can. It's like your heart blocks your brain when it comes to us."

I drop my head into my hands. "If I'm so bad, why didn't you ask for a separation? Why didn't you annul our marriage?"

"When I was alone as a woman in the Gulf, it was easier for me to say 'My husband is a seafarer' than 'I am separated from my husband.' Surely you can understand that."

"But I've never cheated on you!" I blurt out.

"So you were loyal. That doesn't mean that I have to love you."

"But I even got bolitas for you!"

Your eyes bulge. "Why? I never asked you to do that to yourself! Those little metal balls in your—in your—" You can't finish the sentence without gagging.

"I did it because I love you."

"You did it because all of the other seafaring Pinoys do it. If you really cared about what I thought, you'd know I think bolitas are disgusting."

I come closer to you and reach for your hand. "But I *do* care about you. I have loved you and missed you for so long. Come, please, let me show you that I can take care of you."

You hug your arms closer to your chest. "Don't you dare show me those bolitas! And stop promising to take care of me. You don't even know how!" You glare at me, your narrow eyes darker than ever. "It all started when you sent me that stupid hospital package when Nasir was born. I needed nine thousand other things: blankets, diapers, clothes, formula, even *you* at my bedside, but instead, you sent a stupid, ugly, metal Eiffel Tower."

"It showed I was thinking about you—and the baby!"

"Who sends a baby a paperweight with sharp edges?"

Feeling like the breath has been knocked out of me, I put my hands on my heart. "But I sent you love letters, too!" I protest. "I emailed them to you for nine years!"

"They weren't truly for me."

"Of course they were!"

You narrow your eyes, your gaze piercing me so hard that I look away. "Your letters were for a girl—not a mother who had to leave her two sons with her elderly parents in Laoag; not a caregiver who spent years working for families in the Middle East and Canada so her sons could have a better future. You spent nine years writing to a naïve girl—not to a strong woman who learned to write her own story without you in it."

I sink down onto the floor, defeated. "So what do you want me to do? Just disappear? The boys need their father, don't they?"

"The boys need a provider," you reply coldly. "And you know the saying: a good parent is a good provider, and a good provider is one who leaves."

I nod slowly. Every Filipino knows these words; it's practically etched onto the hearts of parents around the globe.

"So go get a good job. One that can actually contribute to the new life we need to build. Find reliable work in a factory, a hospital, a school, a motel, a restaurant. Go somewhere else in the Okanagan if you hate the desert so much. Just go."

You clench your fist to your pinched mouth.

There's nothing left to say.

*   *   *

I stay up all night searching for jobs in the area. Grocery store cashier in Princeton; landscaper in Penticton; tow truck driver in Kelowna—nothing I would ever want to do. By five in the morning, I am blearily considering ads for lumber segment controllers in Quesnel, a town seven hours away. But what if this drought means that the trees burn up in wildfires before I even get there? My eyes start to burn as one question goes through my mind again and again: Why can't we be the perfect family, reunited at last?

Finally, it hits me: you must be in love with another man.

I click on your Facebook profile and sift through the likes and comments under every picture and status update, scrutinizing them for any male names that I don't recognize. I comb through your history for hours, obsessing over how you met this mystery man. Was he working in the Gulf? In Canada? Was he a tourist? One of your old batchmates? A friend of a friend? Have you fallen in love with Erwan, a Pinoy who loves the sand as much as you do?

I try so hard to find the man who has taken my place in your heart, but as I search, the Facebook ads are relentless. "Interac: More fun! More family time! Use INTERAC Debit for the stuff that matters!"; "A&W: Sale on Papa Burgers all weekend long!"; "Whistler Blackcomb Ski Resort: Year-round family fun for all ages!" Every ad has pictures of a happy family that I may never have, even though at this moment, I am closer than I've ever been before.

Through my tears, I see an ad titled "We Need Your Help!" In the video, there's a Filipino child staring at the camera from across the room of a ramshackle little children's centre. With his huge face, messy black curls, and flat brown nose, he looks just like me as a child. But as the camera zooms in, I see the boy lose his temper like a match bursting into flames. The audio is quickly muted as a blond-haired worker tries to read him a book, but he pushes it away, shrieking until he runs out of air, only to scream even louder whenever anyone comes near him.

The camera fades out to a sombre-faced woman sitting primly behind a bare desk. "I'm Miss Forte, a behavioural therapist for this boy and many others like him. For some young newcomer Canadians, this is their everyday reality." The video shows some children playing an English word-matching game with worn-looking laminated paper squares as the little boy stands off to the side, fingers in his ears as he screams at the top of his lungs, his voice muted beneath a sappy music score. "All of our children are special and loved, but for some of them, like this boy fresh from the Philippines, communication is especially difficult. Our centre helps children like little Monolith find their voices. But to do that, we need your help. Please help fund Sunshine Futures today."

As the video finishes, there is a shot of Miss Forte encouraging Monolith to play with the other kids, and the camera pans to a close-up of the boy's reddened face. With his voice muted, I could be imagining it, but I think I can read his lips: "TAMA NA!"—that's enough.

I move closer to the screen as he looks straight into the camera and his words, "TAMA NA! TAMA NA! TAMA NA!", though silenced beneath an inappropriately cheerful ukulele soundtrack, sear through my soul. This child has had enough, and so have I.

I snap the laptop shut. "There's nothing wrong with that boy," I say, pacing around the living room. "He's just angry that he's not back home anymore. Angry that his family is broken. Angry that he's in Canada with no purpose! Isn't it obvious that this is the *real* problem here?"

I peek into our sons' room and I watch them sleeping soundly. They look so peaceful, like they belong here. They're such good boys. Young people make starting a new life look so easy.

I go out the front door. Standing beneath the single waning streetlight, I try to calm myself by conjuring up the happy place that had comforted me for thousands of lonely nights at sea: I'm standing with my arm around your shoulders, kissing your cheek as our sons smile in front of us. We're at a sunny Canadian shoreline, our backs to the glittering ocean, happily reunited at last.

But wait—why have our backs always been to the ocean?

We need to face the water.

Back in Siargao, my elders always swore that water cures everything. When we had scrapes and cuts, they sent us to soak our wounds in the salty ocean waves. Although it burned at first, everything healed twice as fast. As I wipe away my tears, I hear the wise voices of the elders echoing in my head: "There is no wound that the waters can't heal."

As the sun rises over Osoyoos, I walk the two hours along the highway to Spotted Lake.

* * *

I arrive at a strange lake with huge spots across its surface that glitter in the early morning sun. I'd read that the unique minerals and salt crystals turn the spots yellow, green, and blue, but I can't help believing that I'm looking at deep portals to other worlds. The lake is totally still, and as I sit beside a fence, my knees to my chest, I picture what it would look like to be working here every day.

Maybe I would be picking up garbage. Maybe I would be directing cars, repairing fences or handing out pamphlets. If I'm lucky, I would be giving tours. But who would want a tour from a newcomer Filipino who, himself, was just a tourist? The sign says that this is a sacred place for the local Indigenous people. Shouldn't they be the ones working here? Who am I to be representing these waters that don't belong to me?

Spotted Lake is unlike anything I have ever seen. But it's not the ocean. I long for the the cold air, the night winds, the endless horizons.

I walk back to the highway and stick out my thumb, and a huge transport truck pulls over.

"You goin' back to town, buddy?"

I take a deep breath.

* * *

Four and a half hours later, I am in the place that is the most familiar to me in all of Canada: the cruise ship terminal in downtown Vancouver.

The gorgeous building with the high white sails, the seaplanes landing in the water, the crisp air and the promise of the wide, open waters: this is the British Columbia that I know and love.

I race to the edge of the dock and look up at the broad, white side of a Holland America ship. It's too early for cruise season to start, but I saw my old boss post on Facebook that because of the recent storms in the Caribbean, our ships have started coming to Vancouver for repairs before they can be brought back into service.

Using the camera zoom on my phone, I scour every section of the ship until I finally spot a familiar figure doing inspections on the guest room balconies. I'm so excited to see him that my hands begin to shake as I dial his number.

"Hello, Sir Adrian, Sir Adrian! It's Rey! Go out onto the balcony!"

My former boss sees me frantically waving from the railings of the port.

"Sir! Are you hiring? I want to work!"

"Hey, is that the king of the sea, our old Rey Delmar from Siargao? I didn't think I'd ever see you again!" A broad smile spreads across his face. "Some new Pinoy and Indonesian crew members were supposed to start, but their visas didn't come in time. If you come onboard right now, I can get you a contract!"

My heart soars.

As I rush to the ship, I realize that I should phone you and let you know where I am. That I will take care of you and the boys in the best way I know how. That no matter how far away I am, I will always love you.

Instead, I make a quick stop at the post office and send you my newest résumé, which I've updated by hand. In the envelope, I include a little wooden totem pole with the words "With Love from Vancouver" carved along the bottom.

The edges are sharp, but I know you won't mind.

Reynaldo Delmar
rey_del_mar_@yahoo.com.ph

Driver
Aman Family

September 30, 2008–August 2, 2010
Riyadh, Saudi Arabia

**Cruise Ship Employee
(Various Positions)**
Holland America Line

August 30, 2010–February 1, 2019
Worldwide

Cashier
Hello Convenience

March 5, 2019–March 5, 2019
Osoyoos, British Columbia

Jam Seller
Highway 97 Farm

March 6, 2019–March 6, 2019
Osoyoos, British Columbia, Canada

*Cruise Ship Employee
(Position TBA)*
Holland America Line

March 7, 2019–Present
Worldwide

CHAPTER SIX

The Outsiders

Part 1: Avril

WHEN OUTSIDERS FIRST COME to Sarn-hole—that's Sarnia to outsiders—they usually complain about one thing: the air.

"It smells like rotten eggs!"

"It's giving me a headache!"

"It hurts to breathe!"

But one thing about us locals: we don't tolerate disrespect. We know the air smells like sulphur. We know that because of the chemical spills, we have to put up with loud-ass emergency warning siren tests every Monday at 12:30 sharp. But we also know that without the Chemical Valley, we wouldn't have our three-bedroom houses; our trucks and cars; our education; our entire damn lives.

So back in the day, when outsiders used to visit, we'd give them the grand tour. After dark, we'd drive them down to the Valley, when all of the smokestacks were lit up against the night sky, the emissions glowing neon under the flares. We'd take the deepest breath we'd taken all day and say, "Looks just like Vegas, don't it?" None of us had ever been anywhere close to Vegas, but we always swore it must be true.

And if the outsiders even hesitated for a hot second, that was a sign of disrespect. We'd roll down the windows until the outsiders would start to gag on the burning fumes.

Only when they gasped the words, "You're right, it's beautiful, it's just like Vegas!" would we roll up the windows and drive out of the Valley, laughing all the way home.

* * *

I don't need other people anymore. Back in the '90s, we had a Filipino community that was two hundred families strong. There were so many of us that we had our own Pinoy phonebook that the Filipino Association printed especially for us. Whenever we gathered, the parties were huge, filling up an entire park, a community centre, a church hall. It was the best way to grow up.

But decades later, as the titas and titos died of cancer, the only thing that brought our community together was funerals.

So many funerals.

And after every death, more and more of the kids I grew up with moved away. They'd always pull me aside after the service and be like, "Avril, aren't you gonna leave, too? You know it's not safe here, eh?"

But I held my ground. I'd always snap back, "Look, our parents made the ultimate sacrifice so that us kids could build our lives here, and that's worth staying for."

"But there's no one here anymore," they'd yammer on. "You gotta move to a big city, like Toronto, Ottawa, Vancouver—even just London, for Chrissake."

I'd cross my arms tightly. "All of our parents chose *this* city for us to have a better future. They left everything in the Philippines for us to be happy here. You wanna use sob stories about Cancer Valley to get yourself a free-ride scholarship outta here, that's fine. But I ain't disrespecting them like that!"

They'd hug me goodbye, shaking their heads as they walked away.

Even my little brother, Paulo, left me. At first, it was just to do a short program at George Brown College in Toronto. It wasn't available here at Lambton College, so I gave him my blessing. He swore that he'd never leave Sarn-hole for good.

But before he could graduate, both of our parents died. Breast cancer for Mom, pancreatic cancer for Dad.

After we watched Dad's coffin get lowered down beside Mom's still-fresh mound at Lakeview Cemetery, Paulo put his arm across my shoulders and said, "I know Dad split everything between me and you in his will, but I want none of it. I'm giving all of it to you."

My head started spinning. That meant everything would be mine: the old Ford truck with the cassette player that still worked; the huge black leather couch they'd saved up for years to buy at The Brick; the Overlea Crescent townhouse with the view of Confed Street and the Chemical Valley—everything.

"You really want nothing?"

"I'd rather you sell it all and live with me in Toronto," he said. "There are good jobs there. You can do way more than office admin stuff. You wouldn't be alone anymore and—"

I shrugged his arm off of me. "Our parents are barely in the ground and you're already burying them again by taking me out of our home? Are you effing kidding me?"

After that, he never came back to visit, not even once.

*   *   *

But one night, Paulo called me to say that he'd been talking to our family in the Philippines, and that they were gonna ask if they could stay with me while they got on their feet.

"Fine. But when they get here, they better not complain," I said. "I don't wanna hear a single effing word about the smell hurting their lungs or the warning siren tests scaring them shitless. I better not hear them ask, 'OhmyGod, is the water safe to drink or will it mess me up?' None of that, okay? I don't wanna hear them second-guess why out of all of the other places in Canada, our parents picked Sarnia. I'm not gonna give them the opportunity to disrespect me—to disrespect us!"

Paulo heaved a heavy sigh. "Just wait for their text, Avril. And be nice."

"Eff off," I replied. I hung up and cracked open a fresh can of Molson.

*   *   *

Growing up, Paulo and I never had much, but I always knew that we were lucky. Because back in the Philippines, they need friggin' everything.

My mom and dad spent hours at Big V, BiWay, Sears, and Giant Tiger, hunting for things like white Hanes briefs, Always pads, Centrum vitamins, Band-Aids, Kleenex, Spam, and Hereford Corned Beef to send. I remember watching them painstakingly fit the goods into huge cardboard boxes like they were playing Jenga. They'd write a long-ass Taguig, Metro Manila address across the box in a stinky permanent marker, and cover it in so much tape that I swore it could fall from the biggest smokestack in the Chemical Valley and still be intact. They called them "balikbayan boxes," which made no sense to me because "balik" meant "to come back" and "bayan" meant "the country" but there was no way in hell that we'd ever be going back.

By the time I was a teenager, this entire process pissed me off. I'd peek in the box and find they were sending my old clothes that I didn't wear anymore but still loved, like my Gap overalls and my oversized Club Monaco shirts—clothes that took me ages to find at Value Village since fancy stores like that would never open in Sarn-hole.

"Hey! Why are you sending my favourite stuff to them?" I asked, plunging my hands into the box to grab my things.

Mom slapped my wrist and shot back, "It's *your* stuff? Did you buy it with your own money?"

"No."

"Then whose is it?"

"Yours."

"Good. And now that you've outgrown it, I can send it back home." She pointed her lips at my room and I skulked off, slamming the door behind me.

It all came to a head when I spotted them packing up my old toys. I plucked out a plastic bag filled with my Popples and Care Bears and shook it at my parents.

"Who's taking my toys?" I demanded.

"Your Tito Edmond has a girlfriend," Mom replied.

"And she's pregnant!" Dad added. "We need soft toys for the baby."

I made a face. "Edmond's gonna be a father? Wait, he's your youngest brother, right? Isn't he the one who's the same age as me? He's just seventeen! That's so gross!"

"Yes, so technically, he's your *Tito* Edmond, and his daughter will be your cousin."

"Ugh, it's bad enough that I have a tito who's my age. But now you're telling me that I'm gonna have a newborn baby for a cousin? God, that's so trailer trash!"

Paulo appeared in the doorway, holding a textbook. "Can you guys keep it down? I'm studying for my exams."

Bowing down to their favourite child, our parents shooed me out the door.

That was the night I decided to get my first job. I hopped on my rusty Crappy Tire bike and rode straight to Puck Around, the sports bar where folks hung out before and after Sarnia Sting games. I tied up my hair, put on some red lipstick, and stuck out my flat chest as far as it would go. Luckily, they were so under-staffed that I was hired before they even realized that I was still underage. I vowed that, from then on, I'd buy my own shit so that it'd never disappear into a damn balikbayan box again.

But then it got even worse. Instead of shipping off used toys and clothes, my parents started sending straight-up brand-new household items.

"Why does the Philippines get new bedsheets when we've had the same ones since I was born?" I asked. "And how come they get fluffy new towels when ours have holes in them? Why do they get fancy pillows when we've got these ghetto flat ones?"

Mom snapped back, "Your dad and I decided that we will go back to Taguig to retire. So this stuff is for us, too!"

My jaw dropped. "You've gotta be kidding! Why would you wanna do that?"

Dad held the bulging box shut as Mom sealed it with a long strip of duct tape.

"Because that's where home is," she said, simple as that.

My parents had never taken Paulo and me to the Philippines, but we knew two things about Taguig: first, it was a crappy back-water fishing village that sucked away all of our best things, and secondly, after Mom and Dad decided to retire there, her family kept calling to ask for house renovation money like they believed our smokestacks were spewing out hundred-dollar bills. I would constantly fight them on this, saying they should use the money for themselves, but they always said, "We are! We're investing in our future home!"

Too bad our parents didn't live long enough to see it.

Two cancer cases in two years.

Too aggressive to operate.

Too advanced for treatment.

Too late to go back to the Philippines.

It was all too much.

At the end of their days, the doctors told me to just keep them comfortable, but all of our comfortable things were on the other side of the world.

When things got really bad and we realized they wouldn't get better, I asked them if I should buy their tickets to Manila. But they said no, they would rather die at home.

That's when I realized what this Sarnia townhouse meant to them: *this* was their dream home, not some faraway house in a crappy village that they'd worked so hard to get away from. This was the place that they'd made all on their own, with no one to help them. This house was their legacy.

So even after they left me, I swore that I would honour them by staying put.

I wonder what Mom and Dad would think if they knew that the family they'd spoiled for all these years was coming to Canada to suck up whatever they had left?

Effing leeches.

*   *   *

So I got the text message I'd been waiting for. It was Manuela, the girl that my "Tito" Edmond had to marry after he knocked her up a second time.

> Hello I am finished the caregiver program in Alberta
> and got my PR card! I am leaving Calgary and moving to

Sarnla In March. My employers found me a caregiving
job there with their mother! My kids are coming to be
with me and we would be so grateful if we could stay
with you. Monela and Edman are so excited to see their
Ninang Avril!

"Ain't that some shit?" I yelled, my voice bouncing off the walls
of my empty house. "She has the nerve to call me 'Ninang' because
she wants me to act like I'm my own cousins' friggin' godmother?
I never said yes to that, not now, not ever!"

When she gave birth to her second kid, Manuela had called
my mom at two o'clock in the effing morning to ask me and Paulo
to be godparents.

I said no right away. First, I thought it was unbelievably
cringeworthy that Manuela and Edmond decided to do the ultimate Filipino thing and mash their names together to name their
children Monela and Edman. Secondly, they didn't even have the
balls to ask me and Paulo directly.

"Mom, tell them I'm not interested in being a godparent to
these random kids!"

"They're not random—they're family! Don't be disrespectful!"

"Look at what time she's calling you—she doesn't even care
that it's the middle of the night? *That's* disrespectful!"

While my mom and I argued, Paulo used the noisy dial-up
internet to write to Manuela, saying it was an honour to be a
ninong and that he had set up his very first Yahoo email address
just so they could connect.

Model child saved the effing day.

Years later, since my sperm-bank-of-an-uncle couldn't support
his family with just his crappy high school diploma, Manuela went
abroad. She left Taguig and worked in Shanghai and then Calgary
as a nanny, and never went back.

Here's what I wanted to reply:

> Hey Manuela. You popped out two kids as a teenager and
> left them behind to work all over the world while I lived
> with my parents and took care of them till the day they
> died. I sure as hell won't be rolling out the red carpet for
> you guys! You think you can just move in here and take
> over my house? You gotta be shitting me!

Of course, I didn't write that. I live alone in a three-bedroom house, on a street filled with crusty old asthmatics who are just waiting for the day that they'll take a one-way trip to a hospice. So what I actually wrote was this:

> Umm yeah no for sure. You guys can have my guest
> rooms.

Honestly, though, I gotta give her a little respect: Manuela defied all the odds and actually got a job *here*. In *my* town. So many folks are moving outta Sarn-hole like it's under evacuation orders, but here she comes, waltzing in to start a new life and reunite with her teenage kids in a place she's never even seen before.

Maybe Manuela and her kids won't be so bad.

Bah, who am I kidding.

*   *   *

Before they arrive, I walk around the house to decide if I need to clean or not. As I open the creaky doors to my parents' and Paulo's dusty old rooms, I remember the times when the phone would ring in the middle of the night.

I can still hear Paulo, with his bedhead and acne-covered face, shaking me awake so I could messily translate the Tagalog.

Mom: "No no, you didn't wake me up, don't worry. You want money? For what? Okay okay, I'll send it, goodnight, take care, love you."

Dad: "Are you sending your family more money? We already gave them some last month—plus we sent them two balikbayan boxes! What do they want this time?"

Mom: "They need to put a gate and concrete walls on the property."

Dad: "And you said yes? Last time, it was the roof. Then, it was the air-con. Then, new tiles. Where are we going to get the money? We can't keep doing this."

Mom: "We have to! We have a responsibility to my family. Besides, this is the house where you and I will retire someday, remember? I'm doing this for us!"

Then Mom would burst into tears and Dad would storm across the hall and cram himself into Paulo's empty single bed and Paulo would pull out the spare mattress beneath my bed that seemed to be meant just for this purpose and the entire house would hold its breath.

"Sorry I didn't get to the phone before Mom did," I'd whisper to Paulo.

He'd just shrug, take a pill from his secret stash of Gravol, pop it into his dry mouth, and fall asleep.

Eventually, I figured out how to stop the phone from ringing.

After everyone was asleep, I'd crawl military-style across the thick shag carpet in my parents' room and unplug the phone. And in my own room, I'd leave the phone off the hook, so that if anyone called, they'd get a busy signal. It was a relief knowing that nobody could call us at two in the morning to ask for more money that we couldn't afford to give.

I didn't mind falling asleep to the soft beep-beep-beep of an improperly hung-up phone.

It was the sound of peace.

Looking around at the spare bedrooms, I clench my teeth. Who was calling us for money in the middle of the night? Edmond. He rang them up all the time, getting more and more money for anything he damn well pleased.

Edmond and Manuela are the reason my parents used to fight. They're the reason I spent so many years serving cheap beer and gravy-drenched poutine at Puck Around. They're the reason why I settled on an office admin diploma because it was short, sweet, and cheap. They're the reason why my parents died without even a decent pillow to put under their heads.

And starting tomorrow, Manuela and her kids, Edman and Monela, are gonna be living large in my guest rooms like the leeches they've always been. If they're expecting me to lift a finger for them, oh boy, they're outta luck.

I owe them nothing.

Part 2: Monela

WHAT A DISAPPOINTING PLACE.

The streets of Sarnia are nothing like the streets of Taguig. There are no skyscrapers, no greenery, no pedestrians, no traffic, no life. The squat brown-brick buildings look so dated, and I catch myself longing for the modern condominiums and office towers, with all of their steel and shiny glass. I strain my ears to hear something, anything, but the only sound is the cold March wind.

My little brother, Edman, thinks everything is wonderful, of course. He loves the wide roads, the old houses with the icicles dripping from the corners, and the fact that nobody has concrete walls around their homes, making it easy to peer inside. After the Robert Q shuttle dropped us off "downtown," Edman counted the passing cars, laughing that this trickle was considered rush-hour traffic.

At fifteen, he's only two years younger than me, but he already knows that he wants to be a city planner. Whenever we would get stuck in Manila traffic, he would wonder what it would be like if the city were designed properly, so who knows? Maybe this sleepy Canadian city is the perfect place for him.

Ma is thrilled to be here too. From the minute she threw her arms around us at the Toronto airport and welcomed us to Canada with a series of selfies in our new winter gear, she has been so excited to take us to the city where we would start our new life together.

Ma likes that Sarnia isn't trying to be something else. "Back in Calgary, tourists get in their rental cars and buses so they can go to more glamorous places like Banff and Jasper. To them, Calgary is just the beginning of the trip. But in Sarnia, there's nowhere else to go." She points to a building up the road. "See ahead on the highway, where the customs building is? Beyond it, that's the American border. Sarnia is the final Canadian destination!"

In Calgary, Ma finished her first contract as a caregiver, but then her employer asked her to take care of her mother in Sarnia. She immediately said yes since she knew that we already had family to stay with for free. She kept saying how easily everything fell into place, but I don't think this is easy at all.

Back in Taguig, Edman and I had a great life. As developers turned the area around us into a million luxury condos and designer shops, we lived in one of the last old family homes. Papa respectfully rejected all of the developers' offers, knowing that our land would be worth more money year after year. As Taguig exploded, we went from being nobodies to a revered family that business owners whispered about. Our home was tucked away from the street and obscured, first by an old macopa tree that we let grow thickly for good luck, and then by new concrete walls and a big steel gate. The barriers that Papa once built to give Edman and me a safe front yard to play in became the design features that made us look like mysterious old money.

Papa said that if people thought highly of us, we had to look the part. With Ma's caregiving remittances, he eagerly invested in a new car, tailored clothes, skin bleaching, hair rebonding treatments, and more. And of course, Edman and I were sent to the best private schools that Ma could afford.

With the constant flow of Canadian funds from Ninang Avril's generous mother, Papa took advantage of the incredible dollars-to-pesos exchange rate to pay for an entire renovation of the house. First, it was just air-conditioning and hot water and a new roof, but then he got a taste for imported goods. Hand-painted ceramic Portuguese floor tiles, a hand-carved Indonesian dining table, a Japanese toilet with all the fancy buttons—the list went on and on. And when it was all done, he used the rest of the money for the ultimate imported prize: private English tutors so we could master the foreign accent that every Filipino coveted so much.

We stopped speaking Tagalog completely and people started mistaking us for balikbayans visiting from abroad. And when the inevitable day came that Ma sent for Edman and me to come to Canada, Papa was proud of all he'd accomplished. His preparations were done, and we were ready to start our better life abroad.

Or so he thought.

* * *

The little townhouse is only two floors high, with a spindly old tree that looks like a skeleton against the ruddy bricks. It has a screen door that's clinging to the door frame by a single hinge. The early March snow has melted, leaving the shrubs in the garden looking dead, their thin, bare branches exposed to reveal the frozen earth underneath.

As Ma and Edman gleefully snap selfies with the taxi driver and insist on friending him on Facebook, I pull my suitcases up the driveway and step inside the house. I know that I don't need to knock at a place like this.

The floors are covered in a thick, dingy carpet that looks like it hasn't been cleaned in a long time. The living room has a huge black leather couch that's too big for the space and an old television that's half the size of the one we have at home.

I find a set of carpeted stairs leading up to a narrow landing.

"Hello?" I call out.

"Huh, looks like you guys made it," a voice from upstairs replies.

She stands at the top of the steps and I can't help but stare. She looks so sloppy, with her baggy clothes and her terrible posture that makes her half a foot shorter than she really is. Her dry skin looks like it's never been properly moisturized, but her hair is so oily that it looks like she hasn't showered in days. Compared to my father, who is always so put-together, she looks like a whole other species. It seems impossible that we're related.

"I shoulda picked you up from the airport, I know, but it woulda been stupid for me to go gunnin' down the highway all the way to Toronto, what with the gas prices and all. You guys understand, right?"

"Of course," I reply. "The Robert Q shuttle was fine. It wasn't a bother at all, Ninang."

She groans loudly. "Take Paulo's room at the end of the hallway," she says, brushing past me on the stairs.

The bedroom hasn't been used in ages. There's a closet with old green and gold Catholic school uniforms and a set of shelves with outdated encyclopaedias. I pull one out and find compressed Gravol boxes used as bookmarks.

Opening the blinds, I realize that instead of my old view of our lush macopa tree, I now have a horrific view of smokestacks that belch wispy clouds into the air. I'm glad I still have my new winter coat on because this scene makes me shiver. It can't be safe to live this close to a chemical refinery. Canada is supposed to have some of the cleanest air on the planet; the Chinese girls at my private school said that their parents would bring it home in air canisters complete with inhalation nozzles. I make sure that the windows are double-locked and snap the dusty blinds shut.

I just know that this isn't where I'm supposed to be. I'm from Taguig, Metro Manila—an amazing, bustling place where everyone—Pinoy or foreign—wants to be. Sarnia isn't my final destination. It can't be.

*   *   *

Before coming here, all I knew about Ninang Avril was that she was born in Canada, worked at an office, and lived alone in a house where she was letting us stay for free. She sounded normal enough, so I never asked for more information. But in person, there's something about her that puts me on edge.

I poke my head into Ma's room, where Edman is cheerfully helping her unpack her suitcase, oohing and aahing at the Canada-branded hats that she'd brought for us.

"Ma, do you think there's something off about Ninang Avril?"

"Huwag kang mag-alala—don't worry!" she replies, smiling. "You just have to get used to the sarcastic way that Canadians speak."

"Their humour is different from ours?" asks Edman. "I can't wait to be able to tell jokes like a Canadian!"

I roll my eyes and find Ninang Avril in the living room, where she's sitting on the leather sofa, her body sinking into an indentation that looks decades old.

While I watch her gulp down her beer as she intently fixates on a never-ending hockey game, I try to be positive like Ma and Edman.

"I think the name of your city is so pretty: 'Sarnia,' like Narnia, from *The Lion, the Witch and the—*"

"Yeah, yeah, heard that a bajillion times," she says dismissively. "Never even read the damn books. By the way, having seventy-three thousand residents certainly qualifies us as a city, but locals call it a town. Also, we call it Sarn-hole. Not because it's actually a hole, but that's just what you call it unless you're an outsider."

"Sarn-hole." I try to say it politely, forcing a small smile.

Her eyes narrow. "Didn't I just tell you that outsiders can't say that?"

I try another tactic, taking in her saggy black leggings and worn fleece socks. My eyes settle on her oversized red and black checkered flannel shirt. "I like your blouse. It looks very warm. Do you think we could go downtown and find one for me?"

"Downtown? What, you wanna go to Bayside Mall? That place died years ago. They're gonna turn the whole damn mall into a retirement home. Betcha didn't see that coming, but I sure did." She leans forward, her dark eyes boring holes into mine. "No one respects history in this town."

"Maybe there's somewhere else you like to shop?" I ask carefully.

"Value Village," she replies, a smirk spreading across her face.

"There's a shopping village here?" I ask, picturing Bonifacio Global Village, with its pedestrian walkways lined with wide green spaces, glittering lights, and trendy shops.

She takes a long gulp of beer, wiping her mouth with her sleeve. "Value Village is where folks donate the crap they don't want so other folks can get it for dirt cheap."

"That sounds cool," I say, pretending that I'm not dying inside. "Maybe we could go together?"

She eyes my black linen dress, with its crisp, starched collar and pearly buttons. I'd chosen it because Papa always stressed the importance of a good first impression, but now I feel self-conscious.

"I guess you gotta get some normal-looking clothes before you start school after March Break," she says. "You're gonna be an easy target at St. Clair."

"St. Clair? Aren't Edman and I going to Great Lakes Secondary School?"

"That's what it's called now," she says, letting out a dark laugh. "Back in the day, it was St. Clair, after our river, but because the school had a daycare in it, girls got sent there after they got knocked up. So we came up with a better name: 'Skank Clair'!"

Taking in my puzzled face with satisfaction, Ninang Avril turns and goes upstairs to her bedroom. Even behind the closed door, I can hear her cackling.

I haven't heard the term "skank" before. My English tutors never covered terminology like that. I look it up on Google and immediately regret it.

Back home, universities were setting up new campuses all of the time. Just a short drive from our home, I could study at the best law, statistics, and business programs in the entire country. I was living in what the *Philippine Star* said was "poised to become the country's premier 'university city.'"

And now, here I am, across the world, in what may be the biggest downgrade in the history of education.

I text Papa.

> **Monela:** I feel like coming here was a huge mistake. I know you wanted me to finish my last year of high school in Canada, but I would rather be there with you. Can I come back? Please???

> **Papa:** I've been having a hard time adjusting, too. It's so lonely here without you and your brother. But you'll learn to love living abroad, I promise!

Monela: This "better life abroad" thing seems more and more like a myth. Canada isn't better, Papa.

Papa: Your Ninang Avril will take you on a tour of the city tomorrow. Soon, it'll start to feel like home. Stay positive!

* * *

The next day, Edman, Ma and I pile into Ninang Avril's huge, rusty black truck. She's an office worker so I'm not sure why she needs a pick-up truck, but I hoist myself inside and try to stay positive.

As she takes us for a tour of Sarn-hole—I mean, Sarnia— she shows us everything we *can't* see: Puck Around, the horribly named sports bar where she used to work that's now a lounge that's "too damn bougie"; the former Dow refinery where her father worked that's being purchased by a "bunch of shady outsiders from BC"; the site of her old demolished high school, which is now just a sad, muddy field. When she stops in an empty parking lot at Centennial Park, she goes on and on about Filipino Christmas parties that used to be held inside a community centre that has "been bulldozed to smithereens."

And all along the way, she points out the little houses that used to belong to her titos and titas who "bit the big one and peaced out for good."

"What does that mean?" I ask. "They moved away?"

"It means that at our peak in the '90s, we had a big, thriving community. Then we were hit either by cancer or the dumb idea that the grass is greener somewhere else. Anybody new here doesn't know about any of this. They don't even care." Her voice trails off as she glances out the window, a scowl on her face.

I look over at Edman and Ma, who are in their own world, delightedly pointing out the most mundane things.

"Anak, look at how the cars signal to change lanes and stop at all of the red lights!" she says, pointing at the half-empty intersection.

"Wow, Canadians drive like they're being tested by driving instructors!" Edman says, pulling out his phone to take a video.

Finally, Ninang Avril parks the truck beneath a pair of twin bridges that span an icy river separating Canada from the United States. "Welcome to the Blue Water Bridge," she says.

I peer upwards. "But there are two of them—don't you mean the Blue Water *Bridges?*"

"An outsider's mistake," she replies with a huff. "Locals call it 'the bridge.' Singular." She hops out of the pick-up truck with ease.

Ma and Edman immediately start posing for silly Facebook pictures where they attempt to cradle the bridges in their outstretched, mittened hands. Their laughter is so loud that it startles the seagulls, who launch themselves into the air, screaming.

I find a rock that isn't covered in ice and sit down at the water's edge, where the rocks are cut like a giant's staircase leading down to the point where the frigid river becomes a huge lake.

Ninang Avril goes to a food truck with a sign that reads, "Liv'in in the dream Darl'in." I watch in horror as she holds out a box of French fries while the worker liberally spritzes them with clear liquid from a hose attached to the truck's ceiling like he's spraying dirty rainwater all over her fries.

Ninang Avril plops down beside me and offers me some fries. "Doused them in extra vinegar," she says.

I sigh with relief. "No ketchup?" I ask.

She makes a face. "Only outsiders put ketchup on bridgefries."

The fries look perfectly golden and crisp, their steam deliciously rising in the winter air, but suddenly, I'm not hungry.

"I'm sorry that living here is so hard," I blurt out.

She seems taken aback. "I don't want your pity, Monela. Sarnhole's not as bad as you think. You want Indian food or sushi or tacos? Back in the day, it was just Italian and Chinese restaurants, but we got loads of international stuff now. We even had a Filipino restaurant for a little bit, but—"

"But?"

"Well, it died."

I press my lips together.

"Listen, nowadays, we got a great brewery, and hipsters from all over come for our Refined Fool beer," she says defensively. "We got new neighbourhoods, too, with some big-ass houses and everything. And Lambton Mall has fancy brands, like effing H&M. Don't tell me it's not great here."

"But Ninang—"

"You're just a judgmental seventeen-year-old who got here two effing minutes ago. This town was amazing. Still is."

She angrily chews her fries as we sit in silence.

Finally, I work up the courage to ask, "Why doesn't Ninong Paulo live here?"

"After our parents died, he just said, 'I gotta get outta here, Avril. There are too many ghosts.' What a crappy excuse."

"Why would he say that?"

"Okay, you should know that Sarnia is Cancer Alley. Buncha documentary makers and hipster reporters have been poking their noses into our town for ages like they're solving a murder when we all know who dunnit. Lung cancer, colon cancer, pancreatic cancer, you name it and we've had a tito or tita who's died from it. Our mom died of breast cancer—the tumour grew so big and so fast that she died before they could operate, didja know that?"

She looks out onto the lake, which stretches so far that I can't tell where it ends. "After the Dow refinery was shut down, Dad's only happiness was waiting for the Sting to play so he could scan the crowd at the hockey games and see which of his old coworkers were still alive. He never missed a game until the day he left this world, right from that big black couch that he loved. Lost him to pancreatic cancer."

I'm not sure what to say other than three feeble words: "I'm so sorry."

"You don't even know what you really *should* be sorry for," she snaps. "Your dad begged for so much money from my parents. Made our house into a war zone in the middle of the night with the damn phone calls. You made me have to get a job when I was the same age you are now, while I bet you've never had to work a day in your effing life. And all of you knew my parents died and not one of you leeches even called to give your condolences."

"But I didn't—"

"You didn't what? Didn't know, didn't care? The same damn thing happened all over town to two hundred other Filipino families. We're in Canada, where money grows on trees, right? Where you just ask and you get whatever you want, whenever you want it? Sure, the community got decimated by cancer—that's not your fault. But the fact that they couldn't afford the better medical treatments—the fact that all the kids had to clamour for scholarships to get an education—the fact that our parents scrimped and saved just so we could send you the best things—well, that's your fault. Cancer killed them all, sure, but stress killed them, too. I'm tired of your disrespect. We've done way too much for you. Now that you're here, go figure things out for your own damn selves."

"But Ninang—"

"I've never wanted you to call me that, so quit it," she interrupts. "If you gotta call me something respectful, just call me 'Ate.' I'm nobody's effing godmother."

She throws her fries to the screaming seagulls, leaving me alone on the cold rocks.

* * *

When Edman and I were baptized, Mama asked Ate Avril and Ninong Paulo to be our godparents. We received birthday cards, Christmas presents and graduation gifts. Although everything was addressed from both of them, now I realize that all of it was only from Ninong Paulo. He was the one who sent emails on our birthdays; he was the one who called to say Merry Christmas; he was the one who actually wanted to be a godparent. I was so naïve.

I send him a text message.

Monela: Hi Ninong, I'm here in Sarnia. Can we talk?

Ninong Paulo: Hey Monela, my hands are kinda full.

Monela: It's important. Please.

Edman and Ma are sitting together on the black couch, laughing as they upload today's pictures onto Facebook, and Ate Avril is so focused on the hockey game that nobody notices me slip outside and climb into the truck.

My phone lights up with Ninong Paulo's tired face, the worry lines etched across his forehead. Behind him, I notice arched windows with bars on them and faded cartoon posters about sharing and caring.

"Where are you?" I ask. "Are you at work?"

"You guessed right," he replies with a weary smile. He shifts the phone and in his arms, I can see a little boy with a mop of tousled curly black hair across his sleeping face.

"This is my friend Monolith. He just left another centre, and this is his first week with us. He's Filipino just like you." He lifts the boy's limp arm in a wave.

"Should we talk later? Won't he wake up?"

"He's on some meds right now, so he'll be drowsy for awhile."

I straighten up. "What did you do to him?"

He shrugs. "The last centre had his mother get a prescription for drugs that would calm him down, so we're trying them out."

I peer at the sedated boy. "Is this the best way to help him?"

"Right now, it's the only way to keep him from attacking us." He sighs. "His mom doesn't think he's ready for kindergarten yet, so we're making the best of his situation. Anyway, enough about this. What's up with you?"

Unsettled by his directness, I blurt out my request. "Ninong, will you ever come home?"

"I *am* home," he replies. "Toronto's great. You guys should come by for a weekend. I'll take you to the CN Tower, the aquarium, the zoo—wherever you want!"

"You should come home to Sarnia and see Ninang Av—Ate Avril. She needs you."

Ninong Paulo sighs so loudly that his breath moves Monolith's curls. "I keep asking Avril to come and live with me, but she acts like there's an anchor holding her in place. Growing up, Avril had her waitressing gig, so she was always gone. My parents said I was the smart one, so they kept me home to study all of the time. And for what? Our parents died before I could finish school. So after the funerals, I didn't want the inheritance. By the end, they didn't have much money left in their savings, anyway. I let her have everything. I did my part."

The boy in Ninong Paulo's arms begins to shift and I see the big head, the long eyelashes, and the lips frozen into a frown.

"Please, Ninong, you don't understand. It's not about money. I think she needs someone to talk to."

"Isn't that what you guys are there for?"

"She's so angry. I think she needs people who aren't outsiders."

He frowns, his expression perfectly mirroring Monolith's.

"She only talks about places that were demolished years ago— her sports bar, her high school, the community centre. She says we took everything from her, and that the entire Filipino community went through the exact same remittance stress with their own families back home, and this is why she's alone now."

"That's a lot to put on you," he replies. "I'm sorry she said those things."

I notice that he doesn't say that it's not true. I want to say that we never asked for anything, but then I remember Papa's calls to Canada whenever the whim hit him, never questioning if it was the right thing to do.

The little boy's eyes flutter open and he stares at the camera with a glazed look.

"Hey buddy, are you awake already?" Ninong Paulo asks, concerned.

"Hi Monolith," I coo, waving at the screen. "How are you? Kumusta ka?"

The little boy raises his eyebrows and his mouth opens. It looks like he wants to talk, but no sound comes out and he's too debilitated to try. With his chubby hands, he reaches out for the phone as if he wants to touch the screen, but he doesn't have the energy. He slumps forward, his eyes blank and half-closed.

"Monolith, Monolith! Gising na! Wake up!" I tap on my phone insistently. "Ninong, is he okay? Help him!"

"He can't speak."

"Why not?"

"Might be a developmental thing, but it's too early for us to know. Or maybe it's just because he's new here. He and his mom recently moved here from the suburbs in Oakville. Now they live in the Little Manila neighbourhood, so it shouldn't be too bad, adjustment-wise. But who knows, maybe Toronto's too much for him."

I raise an eyebrow. "That's why you think he can't speak? Because he's overwhelmed?"

"Honestly, I can't say. We don't even have enough staff to do a proper assessment. We're just a small centre, and there are a dozen kids who need our attention more. We're all exhausted."

"Did you try singing to him? Or letting him watch a show? What if he doesn't speak English? Did you try speaking to him in Tagalog?"

"I can't speak Tagalog, remember?"

"But why not? Ate said you grew up in a big Filipino community."

His face darkens. "After our parents' generation began to die, us kids all went our separate ways. When I left, I didn't want anything to do with Filipinos anymore. It was too hard." The worry lines on his forehead grow deeper.

I haven't used Tagalog since the English tutors rewired my brain, but in this moment, it all comes pouring out: "Pasensiya na, Ninong. Kailangan ka ni Ate Avril. Please, I know you can understand me. She needs you here. Umuwi ka na."

Monolith blinks his huge eyes open, and his pudgy brown hands reach out to the screen. He locks eyes with me, and his gaze is intense, imploring. I see his mouth open, but Ninong Paulo pulls him back. For a split second, I see Ate Avril in Monolith—the longing for company and love and the cry for help, but without the words to ask.

"Monolith's mom's here to pick him up," Ninong Paulo says quickly. "I gotta go."

I fall back into the truck seat with a groan. I decide to text Papa.

Monela: I can't do this. I hate it here.

Papa: Did you talk to your Ma about it? How is your brother doing?

Monela: He's fine. They're like best friends. Didn't you see it all over Facebook? They're both so happy.

Papa: So why are you upset?

Monela: I don't belong here. Ninong Paulo doesn't even
want to be here—that's how bad Sarnia is. I need to
come back home.

Papa: You know I miss you and I'd welcome you back in a
heartbeat, but your mother worked too hard to bring you
to Canada. Unless you have a really good reason to come
back, you need to stay where you are.

Monela: And what would a really good reason be other
than hating it here?

Papa: Monela, I have to go—but let's talk later, okay?

Dejected, I slip back into the house, where Ate Avril's team
has just won the hockey game. Ma and Edman are jumping up
and down in the living room and screaming "Go Sting go!" as they
record their reactions on Facebook Live.

I look at Ate Avril and for the first time since we've arrived,
she has a small smile on her face.

Taking a deep breath, I ask, "Ate, do you want to go for a
drive?"

*   *   *

The Chemical Valley is so bright at night. With the smokestacks
flaring against the dark sky, the clouds turn into vibrant greens,
yellows, and whites. The stinking refineries that I can see from my
bedroom get closer and closer, but I stay quiet, trying to choose my
words wisely.

"Lemme guess, you don't like it here," she finally says, keeping her eyes on the empty road. "Well then, I'm gonna take you on the grand tour."

She pulls onto the roadside and opens the truck windows, making my eyes immediately water in the acrid air. The smoke-stacks are lined with lights that turn the clouds neon green, the flares at the top glowing so brightly that they hurt to look at.

She watches me intently. "Check out the lights. Looks just like Vegas, don't it?"

Ignoring the stench, I squint a little. "Actually, it kind of looks like Taguig."

She looks at me curiously. "Oh yeah?"

"Taguig is always glittery like this. There are so many tall sky-scrapers that light up the entire sky, so the nights are never dark. It's so beautiful."

Ate Avril frowns. "Skyscrapers? But Taguig is a backwater vil-lage. You don't even have stores."

"We have plenty of stores!" I exclaim. "It's famous for shopping!"

"You're lying. Taguig's a fishing village. That's why my parents had to send so much crap in those balikbayan boxes."

"Well sure, it started out as a fishing village, but that was before Spanish colonization, hundreds and hundreds of years ago. Nowadays, there are new businesses, schools, homes, hospi-tals, universities—it's becoming the pride of Metro Manila." I pull out my phone and show her the shops lining the canal at Venice Grand Canal Mall, the illuminated fountains outside of Uptown Mall, the designer stores and open green spaces on Bonifacio High Street.

She sits back in her seat and slowly closes the truck windows. "But wait—why did you guys take so much of my parents' money if Taguig isn't poor?"

"Papa used their money to renovate the house. He shouldn't have asked for so much from your parents, it's true, but it was also for them, and—"

"I need to take a walk." Ate Avril cuts me off, getting out of the truck to walk along the shoreline. This part of the shore isn't like under the bridge, where the rocks were clean blocks leading down to the lake. Here, they're jagged and foreboding as they lead down to the dark river below. I wonder if she has come here before, in moments of grief.

As I follow her and the biting, pungent winds from the Valley send chills up my shoulders, I long for our gorgeous home filled with art and colour and tropical foliage, nestled between the high concrete walls, safe behind the big steel gate, the perfect hideaway from the noise of the city. I picture myself waking up in my old room, going back to my old private school, getting ready for university. I can see my future so clearly, and I know that it isn't here.

Taking a deep breath, I ask, "Ate, would you ever go to the Philippines?"

"Nope," she replies, shoving her hands into her pockets. "Not interested. I'm good where I am."

"Are you sure?"

She stays quiet for a moment, picking up a jagged rock and clasping it in her hands. "What're you getting at, Monela?"

"I'm sorry that you're alone in Sarnia," I say. "But I just want you to know—this isn't the only home that you have."

"What do you mean?"

"Your parents paid for the renovations of our house. My father always knew that when they retired, they would live with him there. They never got to see the house that they worked so hard to build. But you could."

She casts a sidelong glance at me, her messy bun loosening in the wind. "I can't."

"What's stopping you?"

"I can't leave my job."

"Book a vacation."

"I can't leave my house."

"Ma and Edman will take care of it."

"But I'd be an outsider there," she says slowly. "And everyone knows that's the worst feeling in the world."

"It's not so bad when you have someone to give you the grand tour," I reply, touching her arm.

"What are you saying?" she asks, her eyes guarded.

"I'd love to fly back with you." The words come out of my mouth so fast that I almost regret it.

"Ha, I bet you would."

"No really. I'm serious. I'd help you get settled into the house and show you around every inch of Taguig. I'd re-enroll at my old school. I'd do whatever it takes to make sure that you feel at home."

"You'd do that for me?" she asks, a skeptical look in her eyes.

I nod, flashing her a reassuring smile. "And if you need anything from Canada, you can always ask Edman and my ma to send it to you in a balikbayan box."

As the crisp March winds whip our faces, she breaks into a grin.

"It's the least we can do, Ate."

"Ninang," she corrects me. "Call me Ninang."

CHAPTER SEVEN

The Legacy of Lolo Bayani

Buksan mo ang langit   *Open the heavens*
At kusa mong pakinggan *And listen with purpose*
Ang aking ligalig   *My troubles*
Saka pagdaramdam   *And what I am feeling*
  —KUNDIMAN (ANAK-DALITA)

THERE'S SO MUCH MUSIC.

The happy sounds of the San Marco del Mudo fiesta swirl outside as we watch over the town from the second storey of our bahay na bato, our great stone house. I feel my inay's warm fingers on my wrist, making me wave at everyone calling out to us as I bounce excitedly on her knee.

Our big iron gates are open and people stroll into our home in their finest clothes: the men in crisp, tailored white suits, and the women in their baro't saya, with the long, colourful skirts, the camisa tops made from the finest pineapple fibres, and the panuelos showing off the delicate lace embroidery around their shoulders. The young women gather on one side of our sala, clutching delicate fans to expertly hide a flirty smile for a potential suitor across the room.

My tatay is at the centre of it all, laughing and waving at the growing crowd as he tunes his beloved fourteen-string bandurria. It's an improvement on the twelve-stringed one that the Spanish brought to the Philippines, because, as he says, "The greatness of Filipino songs cannot be contained in only twelve strings, so the Filipinos took their instrument and made it even better!"

"Anak, it's time for you to sing," Inay says as she sets me down, her feather-soft saya de cola tickling my ankles as she swishes towards the piano.

"Is everyone ready for the star of the show?" Tatay calls out. "Please welcome our son, Bayani!"

I eagerly sprint across the polished floors and take my place, standing on a chair in front of the adoring crowd. But when I open my mouth and try to sing, a gust of air bursts out of me, shattering the capiz shell windows, cracking the wooden archways, knocking down the sepia ancestral photos, and splitting the grand escalera mayor in two, the stairs crashing down as they block the corridor. Aghast, the crowd screams and shrieks, rushing out of our bahay na bato, leaving me standing on the chair alone, covered in dust.

*   *   *

What a cruel twist of fate that at the end of my life, my voice has been taken away from me. As I blink my eyes open, I remember that although I'm awake, I remain trapped in a nightmare.

Since I was a boy, my family filled our ancestral home with music. With Inay on the piano and Tatay strumming the bandurria, I would stand on a chair and sing the great Filipino kundiman songs with so much emotion that our audience would be shocked.

"How does the boy sing about heartache so well?" they would ask my parents, eyes filled with tears. "Why can we feel his pain when he has never experienced anything but joy?"

"From the moment the Spanish arrived in the Philippines, they inflicted enough trauma to linger in our bloodlines for generations," Tatay would explain to the crowd, his eyes crinkling with pride. "My son is a descendant of of the Katipuneros of the Philippine Revolution. The ghosts of our ancestors who bravely led the revolutionaries through the towns and forests of the Tagaytay Ridge will never let him forget the weight of the legacy passed down to him. That's why he sings this way. He's our little Bayani—our hero."

Unlike the prominent mestizo families of Batangas province who bragged that they were the descendants of Spanish colonizers, Tatay and Inay were proud that we didn't have a single drop of Spanish blood. We were shorter and darker and poorer than the elites, but still, they flocked to our bahay na bato in San Marco del Mudo to hear us perform. And since we were the descendants of the brave Katipuneros who selflessly fought for freedom, Tatay and Inay declared that we would perform only one kind of song: the kundiman.

"The brilliant Pinoy composers, like Francisco Santiago and Nicanor Abelardo, wrote melodies in the Spanish style that the colonizers loved, but they set the music to our own Tagalog lyrics," Tatay loved to tell us over long, candlelit nights at the dinner table. "See, the Spanish thought the songs were simply about heartache over a woman, when really, they were about heartache over the loss of our country, culture, and identity. The Spanish were so infatuated by the familiar-sounding melodies that they didn't even notice the true purpose of the kundiman: disguised as love songs, they carried hidden messages of the revolution right below the colonizer's noses. Now that's the power of music!"

When I was born, the Philippines was newly independent after decades under American rule. Tatay thought this meant that the Filipino people would long to hear the old kundiman tunes again, but his friends remained enamoured with Western music.

Still, Tatay continued to host the best parties, ignoring the crowd's requests for tasteless American songs.

"After you hear my son sing, you'll forget those colonizers ever existed!" he would declare, beckoning me to the sala stage with a flourish.

I would climb onto my little chair and sing, accompanied by the bright, rhythmic strumming of Tatay's bandurria, and the warm tones of Inay's prized Bösendorfer piano. With a single verse, I could reduce the audience to happy tears as they listened to the old lyrics that they thought they had long forgotten.

I became a master of singing about love gained and love lost. Not only did I become the guardian of the greatest songs in Philippine history, but after my parents, siblings, and wife left this world, I became the sole guardian of our family's legacy, too.

But now, as an old man, my voice is gone. Although my eyes and mind are sharp and my legs and heart are strong, my words only come out in groans and grunts when I try to speak to my caregiver, Tering. And every day, as I lie here in my ancestral home in the shadows of Mount Batulao, I do nothing but wait for death to come for me.

Seventeen years ago, my three children left for their new Canadian homes in Regina and Winnipeg. I have grandchildren now, but they're teenagers who don't even know me.

Tering says that tomorrow, everyone is coming from Canada to see me for my birthday. For the past month, this is all she's talked about. I overheard her as she called them up, one by one, and told them that this will likely be their last time to see me alive. I've tried to tell her that it's already too late—the show is over—but the words are stuck in my throat.

As she bids me goodnight, I desperately try to pass a message to her brain: *They waited too long. Lock the doors.*

* * *

Buksan mo ang bintana	*Open your window*
Tanawin mo't kahabagan	*View with pity*
Ang sa iyo'y nagmamahal	*The one who loves you*
—PAKIUSAP	

"Hell-ooo! Tay! Ta-taay!" The mezzo soprano voice comes floating up from the street. From the sing-song cadence, I know it's my daughter, Franca.

"Tao po? Anybody home?" The warm, dulcet, alto tones definitely belong to my son Rolly.

"Tatay! Ano gaaa?" The booming bass voice comes from my eldest son, Nor. "The door's still locked!"

It's nice to hear their voices again, but I'm glad that Tering locked them out. *How long has it been since my children have paid their respects to this old house, to me? After seventeen years, this is what you get!* I lie back in bed, a satisfied smile on my face.

But then, I hear Tering unlock the heavy iron gate. "Welcome home!" she calls out. "We're so glad you're here!"

My jaw clenches. *Traitor!*

I slowly get up from my bed and watch through a crack in my bedroom door as my children enter the zaguan and climb up the escalera mayor to the sala, lugging their bulging suitcases across the antique narra wood floors where they used to play.

"Clark! Kent! Go wash your hands!" calls Nor.

"Brit-Brit, you too!" adds Franca.

"Eww, we're not little kids anymore—we're teenagers now!" Britney protests.

I wrinkle my nose in disgust. One-hundred and thirty years of ancestors are shuddering from their sepia portraits on the walls, horrified to hear their descendants speaking English in this ancestral place. *Is this our legacy?* they ask.

Tering shows Franca and Nor to their old bedrooms. The parents are the ones hauling the suitcases, while the kids, with freshly washed hands, slump down onto the rattan chairs, their eyes on their phones.

"Anyone got the internet password?" Kent asks.

"Hey Terry?" Britney calls out, carelessly anglicizing Tering's name. "Wi-Fi actually exists here, right?"

Clark saunters into the kitchen and comes back with a bottle of Coca-Cola, helping himself as if he's been here before. "Wow, good thing we ate at the McDonald's on the highway. That fridge smells like something died inside of it."

"Maybe it's Lolo!" Kent retorts, stretching across the mahogany day bed, his shoes dirtying the hand-woven sulihiya. "Check to see if his head's in there!"

Walang respeto! I seethe, narrowing my eyes at my towheaded grandson.

Where are Rolly and his daughter? I wonder. *The half-Black one?*

Rolly slowly comes up the steps and enters the sala. My youngest looks so different now: soft paunch around his waist; receding hairline; a pair of thick glasses on his sweaty, round face.

"Philippa, sweetheart, are you sure you're okay with the luggage?" he calls out.

A lilting soprano voice echoes from below, sweetly bouncing off of the stone floor. "Oh, relax! It's not that heavy!"

Rolly sinks down into his old favourite tumba-tumba chair and rocks back and forth, his body at rest, but his concerned eyes scanning the room. Suddenly, I see everything through him: the water-stained wallpaper; the warped ceiling fans; the damaged weave of the rattan chairs; the cracks in the beams; the dust that has settled into every hand-carved archway, onto every picture frame, inside every crack and crevice. For the first time in my life, I'm embarrassed by my own home.

Why didn't Tering clean more? I wonder. *Why didn't she polish anything? Why didn't she get anything repaired?* On days when

I felt well enough to walk around the house, I caught her playing Mahjong or Pusoy Dos with the maids next door or watching
teleseryes in her quarters. *So lazy!*

Even her food had gone downhill. While she used to painstakingly decipher our old family recipes for lomi and bulalo written
in the spindly penmanship of my childhood yaya, lately, she would
only make a tired lugaw, a bland rice porridge topped with only
a few pieces of chicken and some pieces of ginger—just enough
sustenance to make me live through another day.

She wasn't the best caregiver, that was for sure. No formal
training, no education—she was just a simple woman who'd lived
her whole life in a shack at the edge of the kapeng barako farms.

But in my time of need, she was all I had.

"Tita Tering?" Rolly calls out, his voice strained. "Where's
Tatay?"

"He's in his room. He's still asleep."

"Pwede po ako sumilip? Can I see him?"

"Pwedeng pwede, Sir Rolly, of course."

Hurrying over to my bed, I lie down, close my eyes, and
breathe as deeply as I can.

Rolly comes into the room, sighing softly. "You're sleeping
with your glasses on," he whispers, gently slipping them off and
putting them on my bedside table.

He puts his cool hand on my forehead. "Naandito ho kaming
lahat—everyone's here now—well, me, Nor, Franca, and our kids.
Pasensiya na Tatay, Tita Tering's invitation was so last-minute that
our spouses couldn't take time off, but I don't think you'll mind,
right? We're so excited for your birthday party tomorrow. We can't
wait to celebrate with you. Rest muna, okay? Love you." He presses
his nose against my cheek and sniffs my skin, and my heart melts,
just a little.

Rolly, my favourite.

If only he hadn't left me in the first place.

*　　*　　*

Kung nais malaman Sinta	*If you want to know, Dear*
Bakit tangi kang minamahal	*Why you're the only one I love*
Ikaw lang ang tunay at	*You are the only*
siyang dahilan	*true reason*
Ng aking kaligayahan	*For my happiness*
Minamahal, minamahal kita	*I am loving you*
Pagsinta ay di magiiba	*My love for you will never*
	change

—MINAMAHAL KITA

This bahay na bato has always been a place of magic. Our sala mayor became the province's best place for tertulias and bailes—the parties and dances that stretched long into the night.

Even as a young man, when my friends only wanted to hear songs played by bands from some faraway Woodstock festival, I still performed the old kundiman songs. I could sing "Pamaypay ng Maynila" and turn the most demure wallflowers into waltzing ingenues, making them flutter their fans to my three-quarter beat. I could sing "Minamahal Kita" and make the most obstinate bachelors extend their hands to the women who would soon become their wives. Beneath the capiz-shell lanterns and candelabras, I could put everyone under a spell that made people dance, sing, fall in love, and remember the past—even when they were wearing polyester bellbottoms.

My heart longs for that magic again. I wish my estranged grandchildren could experience it. If only I could loosen my frozen tongue and sing the songs that are theirs by birthright.

When everyone is asleep and the house is quiet again, I sit up in bed and try to sing. I fill my lungs up and try to make a sound, but only one syllable comes out: "Pa! Pa! Pa!" I start to cough and hack, my lyrics reduced to laboured breaths.

Tering sleepily rushes in, her greying hair askew and her eyes half-closed.

She hands me a glass of water.

"Paaa!" I say, pushing the water away, annoyed. "Paaa!"

"I know, you want your Papa," she says, yawning. "If you call him, he'll come for you soon, maniwala po kayo."

I'm not calling my father, I tell her in my mind. *He's never been "Pa," but "Tatay."*

It's just that I can't make any other sound come out.

*   *   *

Irog! Masdan mo ang pagtangis	*Beloved! Look at the mourning*
Ng abang pusong api sa pag-ibig	*Of a humble heart that is deprived of love*
Tanging lunas na nga lamang	*The sole remedy then is that*
Dilag moy masilip	*I see your magnificence*
At itataghoy-taghoy	*And that I bemoan*
Ang mga pasakit na tini-tiis	*The suffering that I endure*

—IKAW RIN!

Every kundiman song has the same pattern. It must start out with sadness, with the singer filled with heartache and longing as they suffer to prove their undying love. This is why the songs always start off in a minor key, so the anguished lover can show the extent of their despair.

But just when all seems lost, the song shifts to a major key, and suddenly, anything is possible: abundant joy, true love, eternal happiness. The singer's voice soars as the music swells to a crescendo, making the audience giddy with the possibilities of all that could be. They finish the song believing in the happy ending that everyone dreams of.

In my youth, I wanted to sing only the major-key verses so that the dancers would be joyous and twirl around the room, but Tatay stopped me with a sharp squeeze on my shoulder. Pulling me in close, he said, "If you stray from the minor-major formula, this is not a kundiman. You cannot have joy without sorrow. How can you appreciate happiness when you haven't suffered first?"

Oh, how my descendants have made me suffer. Initially, I was happy that Nor and Franca finished their studies in Canada and then married their Filipino-Canadian sweethearts—and best of all, not ones with Spanish surnames, but proud, local Filipino names that withstood colonization: Katigbak and Masangkay. But when Nor told me that he'd named his boys Clark and Kent after Superman, and Franca admitted that Britney's name was inspired by some American pop star, I let them drift away from me. I'd named my own children after the kundiman legends Nicanor Abelardo, Francisco Santiago, and Ruben Tagalog, but they dishonoured our legacy with meaningless names.

I never forgave myself for letting my children move to Winnipeg and Regina. I should have known that in these selfish times, international students would never come back to the Philippines. Naïvely, I thought they would be like the Ilustrados, going abroad to expand their ideas of democracy and justice, and then coming home to inspire a revolution. But instead of becoming the José Rizals of their generation, they settled into their comfortable new Canadian lives, turning their backs on the country that had nurtured them.

But now that their children are here for the first time, perhaps I can help them experience the magic that they have missed.

* * *

In the morning, I wait by the crack in my bedroom door and wonder if any of them will go to Inay's Bösendorfer piano. In the 1800s, it was brought from Austria to the Philippines for the home of a greedy Spanish friar. When he fled our town during the revolution, my forefathers claimed the piano for the Filipino people, bringing it home to stay here forevermore. In the entire country, there are only nine left. And out of those nine, I wonder how many of them are like ours, waiting for glory once more?

I left the piano lid open with Inay's yellowed old sheet music on display. It would be the high point of my final days if just one of my grandchildren showed any interest in a kundiman. After only a few bars, I just know that it would awaken the legacy that lies dormant in their blood.

Soon, Britney comes into the sala, her sparkly pink phone high above her head, her long black hair swishing against her back.

"I'm telling you guys, the internet doesn't exist here!" she says, pouting as she collapses onto a rattan chair that catches on her alarmingly tight sundress.

Tering sighs as she comes out of the kitchen, holding a serving platter loaded with homemade pandesal and hand-ground peanut butter. "It exists, but it's just slow," she replies, gritting her teeth. "I can hire a tricycle to drive you to the internet café."

Britney wrinkles her nose. "Is that the place we drove past with all of the walls painted black and the sweaty gamer-boys inside? Eww!"

Tering sighs and retreats to the kitchen.

Clark and Kent enter the room in loose jerseys and shorts like they're ready to play basketball. Clark grabs a fresh pandesal, spilling breadcrumbs all over the floor as he mocks his cousin. "OhmyGod, gamers are sooo gross!"

"Wait, did she say a tricycle?" Kent asks. "Like the bike for little kids? Why would she hire a baby to take us somewhere?"

"I think she means those deathtrap motorcycles with a passenger cab that's so low you're at ankle level with the driver," Clark replies. "Imagine those in a Prairie winter!"

"Guys, I just wanna go to a resort," Britney whines. "This place was kinda cute at first in like, a vintage way, but it doesn't have A/C so it was boiling in my room all night, and then this morning I tried to take a shower, but the water was freezing because there's no hot water! I'm either too hot or too cold and my skin just can't deal with this!"

"Yeah, let's get outta here," says Clark. "I wanna go to a resort gift shop and buy a belly song."

"Uhh, dumbass, I think you mean a balisong," Kent replies, pretending to stab his brother with a butterfly knife. "And I'm pretty sure you won't be allowed back to Winnipeg with a legit weapon in your backpack."

"Ohmygosh, is that a baby lizard on the wall?" Britney exclaims, jumping out of her chair as a harmless brown butiki scurries behind a curtain in pursuit of a mosquito. "Why aren't there screens on the windows? I'm sooo done here!"

Franca comes into the sala, ignoring the pandesal. "You're right. We should go to a resort. Batangas province is full of beautiful places that you'd all love."

"But we're here to celebrate Tatay's birthday," Rolly protests, coming into the room with a bimpo on the back of his sweaty neck. "It might be his last one. Look, I know this isn't what you guys are used to back home on the Prairies, but—"

"Tito Rolly, this is, like, two thousand times worse than the Prairies," says Britney. "Regina looks like Disneyland compared to this. I'm sooo ready to go back to Saskatchewan."

"You kids just need some time to adjust," Rolly says. "How about your Tita Franca brings all of you to a resort for a day of swimming and high-speed internet and souvenir shopping while your Tito Nor and I take care of things in the house?"

"What things?" Nor asks, examining the expiration date on a bag of kapeng barako and throwing it into the garbage. "I think you can see the state of things." He gets up and tries to open a sliding ventana, but it's stuck in place and covered in a layer of street soot that turns his hands black. Turning to Clark and Kent, he says, "Boys, let's go."

Franca turns to Britney. "Sweetie, get your phone charger and some sunscreen. We'll call a car to take us to Tagaytay."

"But wait—" Rolly begins, but he's interrupted when Nor sharply closes the lid of Inay's piano.

"This isn't the same place we left behind. It's time to let it go."

Soon, the house is silent again, except for the sound of Rolly's heavy sigh.

*　*　*

I miss being invited to sing.

At the fiestas, I would lead the entire barrio in song after song, my voice echoing through the plaza. At weddings, I would perform the newlywed's first dance. At the cathedral, I would lead the hymns and bring people closer to God. Where there was a crowd and a live band, I was always given a place of honour and asked to share my gift.

Then, it was all taken away from me.

It's a fact that Filipinos love karaoke. While it's one thing to perform onstage in front of a crowd, it's another thing altogether when families would save their pesos to buy a karaoke machine so they could sing into the night. No more live instruments in a rondalla, no more dancers in their finest clothes, no more romance and magic. A night of music was reduced to a flickering screen with often misspelled lyrics flashing across it, the songs paired with unrelated videos of European girls wandering around cobblestone streets, doing their best to look beguiling and contemplative as they waited for lovers who were never, ever Filipino.

The only time I was handed a karaoke microphone, I was walking past a party on the outskirts of town. There were people playing cards as they ate balut and drank Red Horse and lambanog. Eager to christen their new machine, the audience egged me on. "Come on, Lolo Bayani! Get the high score!"

I leafed through the songbook. "Where are the kundiman?" I asked.

"Nobody sings kundiman anymore," they hollered. "Just pick an American song, Lolo!"

I set the microphone down. "Music is dead," I declared. "I'm going home."

As I trudged home with a dark cloud in my heart, a woman I recognized from church hurried out of her shack on the edge of the coffee farms. She was wearing a simple floral duster and a pair of worn tsinelas, and as she approached, her frizzy, greying hair blew in the wind.

"My late husband, bless his soul, always said that when you sang at mass, it was the only time that he felt close to heaven," she said, smiling at the memory. "Even during his last breaths at the hospital, he could hear your voice echoing from the church, and he closed his eyes in peace. Please, sir, I don't have much, but please accept my gratitude."

Taking in her earnest smile, I felt suddenly lightheaded. "I really needed to hear that today," I said. "Thank you for sharing this with me."

I reached out to shake her hand, but before our fingers could touch, my world went black.

*   *   *

Kung sa tapat ninyo	*If in your path*
Magdaan ang bangkay	*You come across my corpse*
Makipaglibing ka	*Please bury me*
Ikaw ay umilaw	*Light a candle*
Ako'y ipagdasal, ako'y	*And pray for me, and pray*
ipagdasal	*for me*
Pa-alam! Ay! Pa-alam!	*Farewell! Ah! Farewell!*

    —PAHIMAKAS

The sounds whirled around my ears: the beeping of machines, a pen scratching across a clipboard, a teleseryes blasting from the television in the next room, and two strange voices above me.

"Are you his wife?"

"No Doctor, my name is Tering. I saw him in the street. You know he's a famous singer?"

"Was he drinking?"

"No, I don't think so."

"Do you think he has money to pay for a hospital bill?"

"I know he lives in that old bahay na bato in the centre of town. He must have some money."

"Does he live alone?"

"I think he's a widower."

"He'll need constant care after this. He won't be able to speak or do anything on his own for the time being—or maybe forever. Do you think his children will help?"

"I think they all live abroad."

"Ahh. Typical."

"Doctor, what can I do?"

Call Rolly, I wanted to say. *My son Rolly works as a caregiver for seniors in Winnipeg!*

I tried to speak but my lips wouldn't move. I tried to raise my arms but it was impossible. It was like my entire body was frozen.

The woman cleared her throat. "I'm the last person he spoke to. I believe that God sent me to take care of him. Hindi ko siya pababayaan. Don't worry, I won't leave him alone."

I sighed with relief. My body had betrayed me, but at least there would be someone with me when I died.

*   *   *

Kung tunay man ako	*To show that I'm sincere*
Ay alipinin mo	*I'll be a slave for you*
Ang lahat sa buhay ko'y	*Everything in my life is*
Dahil sa 'yo	*Because of you*

—DAHIL SA IYO

Tering moved into my bahay na bato with delight.

"I've always wanted to go inside one of these old houses!" she exclaimed.

Immediately, she went to work, tidying up the house for the first time in years. When my wife, Liwayway, died, I dismissed all of our helpers so they wouldn't remind me of her, and the house looked like it had grieved along with me. Tering opened all the windows to let in the fresh breeze blowing up from the cliffs, swept every corner clean of dust and cobwebs, picked fresh sampaguita from the bushes and strung them into garlands to hang in every room, and polished each gilded frame that held the sepia photos of my departed relatives, commenting on how striking each of them was.

Tering took care of me like a child. She bathed me, fed me, changed me, and brushed my hair and my teeth. And over time, my wounds healed—the outside ones, anyway. Eventually, I learned to sit upright, to move around slowly, and to take out my wallet every week to pay her for the constant care. When I wanted to talk to her, I'd reach for a pen and paper, but my shaking hands made it impossible to write.

"Don't write to me," she told me one day. "You used to be the most famous kundiman singer in all of Batangas. I know you could speak if you just tried harder."

I tried as hard as I could, but still, nothing would come out.

Tering thought I was just being stubborn. "Sira ka talaga," I heard her mutter when she thought I wouldn't hear.

And she was right; without my voice, I truly felt broken.

I remembered that the meaning of the word "kundiman" is "if not meant to be." *Kung hindi man.* It's a way to accept that things may not work out, no matter how much you want them to happen.

Perhaps getting my voice back wasn't meant to be.

With tears in my eyes, I reached for my favourite barong Tagalog that I had used for hundreds of performances, and laid it on my bed. Woven with fine, translucent pineapple fibres, the material was so delicate that it suddenly reminded me of the skin of an old man who was ready to die.

"Is this what you want me to bury you in?" she asked.

I nodded.

* * *

One morning, I awoke to a strange child in my room. When I saw him, I wasn't startled as much as I was curious. His massive hands and head made him look like a cartoon.

"This is Monolith, my only grandchild," Tering announced as the child darted behind my bedroom door. "His papa, my son-in-law, is a good-for-nothing, violent drunk, and his guardian, my daughter Sora, can't care for him while she's taking her science exams in Los Baños. So he will join us here."

I raised my eyebrows to ask, "Where is his mama?"

Somehow, Tering understood. "His mama is in Hong Kong, but soon, she'll be moving to Oakville, Canada." She plucked the boy out from behind the door and brought him to the foot of my bed.

I stared at him intently, desperately trying to tell him, "I know what it's like to have family in Canada. I know what it's like to be left behind." But the boy looked away.

"He's not like a regular child. He's like you. He won't talk. Nobody knows why." Tering laughed. "Hey, isn't it funny, the two of you mutes living in San Marco del Mudo, a town named after St. Mark the deaf-mute? You'd think there was something in the holy water!" Shaking her head and chuckling, she handed him a glowing screen. "Here's your iPad, Monolith. Show Lolo Bayani how it works. Keep each other company while I go to the market, okay?"

When she left, Monolith poked my feet, my side, my arm, my cheek, as if he was trying to test me. I was so exhausted that I just lay there and watched, amused. Finally, he climbed onto my bed and turned the iPad on, his screen lighting up my room. At first, he faced away from me, hunching over the iPad, but when he saw me craning my neck to see what was on the screen, he tilted it to face me. I liked the bright colours and the upbeat soundtracks, but the English storylines made me lose interest. I quickly fell back asleep.

When I awoke to the warm pink and golden tones of sunset filling the house, I gestured for Monolith to put the iPad down. As I slowly shuffled to the sala, he reluctantly followed me to Inay's grand piano. In my past life, I would've told him that its rarity was only matched by its exceptional tonal quality, but instead, I just motioned for him to press his fingers to the keys. With such chunky hands, I thought he would do as most little boys do and wildly mash the ivories until I pulled him away, but instead, Monolith pressed the highest key over and over with great timidity, like he was too scared to make a sound.

Motioning for him to stand on the piano bench, I slowly opened the heavy wooden lid to let him see the little hammer softly hitting the string inside as he played. As I lifted the dusty lid, it made a loud click-click noise, which snapped him to attention.

Then, he did something I'd never seen any child do: he eagerly plunged his big head into the innards of the piano, reaching down and plucking the tiny strings by the tuning pegs. Filling the house with his strange diwata harp sounds, he grabbed my arm and put my hand inside the piano, and together, we filled the house with the oddest, most beautifully dissonant music that these walls had ever witnessed.

"What's going on here?" Tering's voice rang through the house as she ran up the stairs, scattering vegetables all over the floor. "Monolith, what are you doing up there? Anak ng demonyo! You'll break your Lolo Bayani's bench!"

Monolith began to make a wailing sound, and I gestured emphatically to let her know that it was my idea.

"Oh, no, no, none of this from you mutes! Both of you, go to your room!"

She led us back to bed, grumbling as she left.

Monolith sank into the space beside me, snuggling at my side with a contented sigh.

* * *

Kung ako'y mamamatay	*If I am to die*
Sa lungkot niaring buhay	*Of sorrow in this life*
Lumapit ka lang	*Come near to me*
Lumapit ka lang	*Come near to me*
At mabubuhay.	*And I will live.*

—MADALING ARAW

It felt wonderful to have a little boy in the house again. He reminded me so much of Rolly.

Rolly, my youngest, my beloved bunso, the last of my children to leave me. Franca and Nor both went to Canada as international students—Franca to the University of Regina, and Nor to the University of Manitoba. But Rolly swore he would never study abroad, promising to fill our house with music and laughter forever. Not only did he love all of the kundiman, but he had inherited the best of my family's musical skills: he could play the piano and the bandurria with both Inay and Tatay's legendary flair, and with his smooth alto voice, he could sing in perfect harmony with me. Everyone marvelled at how he was the perfect child to inherit our family's legacy.

But then, he fell in love with a Black girl from Winnipeg.

Liwayway and I were against it from the start.

San Marco del Mudo rarely attracted foreigners; they usually skipped over our simple town to explore more famous Batangas attractions with slogans like "Anilao, the birthplace of Philippine scuba diving" or "Tagaytay, the island within a lake within an island" or "Taal, the Heritage Town." We had no interest in tourists.

But Rolly insisted that Rebekah wasn't a tourist. She had paid an enormous sum of money to come to the Philippines to work for free in the orphanage, painting walls and playing games with the kids.

We were immediately suspicious. "Who would pay to come all the way across the world to work for no pay?" Liwayway asked him. "She must have bad intentions."

But Rolly wouldn't hear any of our protests. For the first time in his life, he was in love.

He earnestly brought Rebekah home to meet us, but we weren't interested in sharing a meal with her, no matter how much Rolly pleaded. One night, they even came over with a strange-smelling platter of rice and peas. Rebekah set it down on the table, shyly saying that her mother had mailed the ingredients just so she could make this Jamaican dish properly for us. We let her dish grow cold in the middle of the table as we silently ate our plain white rice, ignoring Rolly as he tried to convince us that her spicy rice was better than anything he had ever eaten before.

That night, we overheard him meeting her mother—a woman who came to Canada from the Caribbean as a domestic worker in the 1980s—over a video call. Rolly left his bedroom door open so that we could hear how welcoming she was, saying sweet things like, "I'm so thrilled to meet you"; "You're a gift from God"; "Thank you for making my daughter so happy." Rebekah and Rolly had barely started their courtship, and already, he was receiving warmth like this? Did she not want her daughter to marry someone from their own community? Liwayway and I became even more suspicious of Rebekah.

Unable to understand our concern over his first love, Rolly dipped into his savings and paid for a room at the orphanage workers' dorm so he could spend all of his time with her until her contract was finished. The entire town was aghast at the scandal.

After Rebekah left for Winnipeg and he came home to us, we thought our troubles were over, but our son was lovesick. He applied as an international student at the University of Manitoba, where Rebekah, her mother, and his Kuya Nor were already waiting. And when he was accepted on a full scholarship, he left us in the middle of the night—no despedida party, no special mass, no last hugs, no final song to say goodbye.

The emptiness he left behind consumed the entire house.

* * *

Di baga sumpa mong   *Did you not promise*

Ako'y mamahalin?   *You will love me?*

Iyong itatangi, iyong itatangi   *You would set me apart, you*

Magpa-hanggang libing   *would set me apart*

Subalit nasaan ang gayong   *Until death*

    pagtingin? *But where is your gaze?*

Nasaan ka Irog?   *Where are you, Beloved?*

    —NASAAN KA IROG?

Soon after Rolly arrived in Winnipeg, Nor called us to demand that we send money.

"Your golden child screwed up," he said. "Rebekah's pregnancy test just turned out positive and Rolly's dropping out of school to support her. They're getting married soon. Better send two presents: one for the wedding, and one for the baby."

Liwayway and I couldn't believe it. Our bloodline was a mix of great Filipino revolutionary heroes and artists. Sure, there were also gamblers, drunkards, and the odd crooked politician, but that was normal in any storied family. We were so proud of our lineage, and it certainly didn't have any room for a Filipino-Jamaican grandchild in Canada. And for Rolly not to tell us any of this? It showed how little he respected us now, because of this woman who had stolen him from us forever.

A few months later, Liwayway had a heart attack and died in her sleep. Heartbroken and horrified as I woke up beside her lifeless body, I called Rolly for the first time.

When he answered the phone, he was already crying. I was touched that after all of our months apart, he was still so psychically tethered to me that he already knew what had happened.

But as he blurted out his announcement, I realized that while I cried tears of misery, his were tears of joy.

Philippa was born.

*   *   *

Puso ko'y lunod na	*My heart drowns*
Sa dagsa ng hapis	*In the torrent of anguish*
Saan kukuha pa	*How much more*
Ng pagtitiis?	*Can I endure it?*

—HIMUTOK

To support his new family, Rolly found a temporary job as a caregiver for seniors. He began to phone me a few times a year, whenever looking after Canadians made him feel guilty for being away from me.

"As soon as I save enough money, I'll come home to see you," he would promise.

But as the years went by, I lost hope.

Then Franca got married, followed by Nor—both to Filipino families who had already been in Canada for two generations, so there was no question that they would stay in Regina and in Winnipeg. I couldn't bring myself to travel alone to see them, and they never wanted to come back to see me. I stopped the expensive upkeep of the house. The townspeople whispered that our crumbling property would one day be demolished or turned into an underfunded museum, but I didn't care.

My legacy was dead.

But then Monolith moved into my home—and into my room, as he refused to sleep anywhere else.

We spent hours playing blinking games, making funny faces, and tickling each other's feet as if we were daring the other to speak first. And if I needed to rest, he turned to his iPad. When he started watching his shows, nothing could distract him—not even the strange green picture of a telephone that would flash across the iPad screen with the words "Mama Vera." Sometimes, a voice would fill the room, saying in English, "Hello, Monolith, are you there? My camera is broken, so I have no video, but can you hear me? Hello?" Annoyed, he would just press a red button and go on with his beloved cartoons.

Soon, I started to see a pattern: a pack of dogs on rescue missions, a schoolhouse for mer-children, a precocious British piglet—the shows were charming, but the characters never spoke anything but English. *Were there no more local cartoons being made?* I wondered. *Filipinos are creative people; don't we have some of the top animators and storytellers in the world?*

I realized that someone must have chosen these shows for him, as if Monolith was being trained to live abroad someday. It must have started with his silly English name—why else would a country girl name her child "Monolith"? Did his Mama Vera think that she was being clever by giving him an English name that no Westerner would ever consider? Or did she just think that even the most random English word was better than our proud Tagalog names?

This is the end of our cultural legacy, I thought. *When language dies, how will we remember who we are?*

I used to mourn that the old-style Tagalog from the kundiman lyrics had already been dropped from common parlance, only to be replaced by simpler Tagalog—or worse, bastardized Taglish—that lacked the musicality and complexity of our original words. But looking at Monolith, I mourned something deeper: that he was being taught that the only language he needed to learn was English—a confusing, isolating thing to do to a child growing up in a rural Tagalog town.

No wonder he doesn't speak. He doesn't know who he is.

With Monolith snuggled at my side, his iPad lighting up his young face, I realized that this had to end with me. I had revolutionary blood in my veins; I could save our legacy. I could make him love the words that his generation would soon forget.

I had to try to speak again.

When Tering came into my room to fetch my dirty clothes, I gathered up my strength.

"Pa," I said, my voice barely a whisper.

"Look at all of this tubal," she muttered to herself. "For an old man who doesn't go anywhere, you think he'd have less laundry, putris."

"Paaaa," I begged, waving my hands in the air to get her attention.

She looked at me, eyebrows raised. "Wait—you can make sounds now? Very good! Are you trying to tell me something? Sige, try!"

I want a party. I want to hire a pianist, a bandurria player, and a singer to perform my favourite kundiman. I want Monolith to hear the old Tagalog words. I want him to experience the beauty of his ancestral language. He needs this. I need this. Please, Tering, let's have a party like the ones this house used to have.

I motioned for her to bring my calendar to me. "Pa?"

Following my finger, Tering saw that I was pointing to a specific date. "Do you want to have a birthday party?" she asked, a smile spreading across her wide, wrinkled face.

I threw my head back onto my pillow, nodding with relief.

"What a fantastic idea! I'll invite all of your children—I'm sure they'll come back to see you. You're right. This might be your last birthday on this earth—it's time for them to come home!"

I shook my head emphatically—"Pa pa pa!"—but in her excitement, she had already left the room.

I heard her call up Nor, Franca, and Rolly and eagerly convince them to come home for my birthday before it was too late to say goodbye. I didn't have the words to protest. All I could say was "Paaa!" and furrow my brow, making her laugh and say, "Yes, you'll see all of your children and grandchildren soon! Aren't you excited for your party?"

I turned over in bed to face the wall. A birthday party with my children was the last thing I wanted.

* * *

As my birthday approached, I had trouble sleeping, and I noticed that Monolith did, too.

He whimpered in his sleep, covering his ears with his giant hands as if to block a round of blows. He lashed out with his chunky feet, limbs flying everywhere, kicking pillows and blankets all over the floor and crying out like he was being hurt. Tering would come rushing in to rouse him out of his sleep, putting the iPad in his hands to calm him down.

"Here Monolith," she would say, half-awake. "Go watch your English shows."

One night, after he fell asleep mid-cartoon, I saw the strange green message flash across his iPad: "Mama Vera." Curious, I tapped it with my shaking finger.

"Monolith? It's me—it's Mama! Are you there?" The woman's voice flooded the room, making it hard for me to breathe. "I just sent your Tita Sora the plane tickets, okay? Are you excited? You'll finally be coming to live with me in Canada!" Her soprano voice sounded sweet and earnest, but my heart sank.

I quickly pressed the iPad again, making the screen go dark.

I felt so helpless, so livid, that this little boy whom I had come to love as if he were one of my own would disappear like all of my children. Another Filipino lost to the Western world, where English was the language of progress, abandonment, erasure. Monolith's ancestral Tagalog, and all of the culture and history and heroism and nuance and musicality that came with it, would be a legacy that he would one day forget.

* * *

The day that Monolith's Tita Sora finished her exams, she came to my room to collect him. She had a big backpack on her shoulders, and she looked so tired that her glasses seemed to magnify her lack of sleep. She wore a rumpled polo shirt and jeans, and her long hair was tied up in a bun that was falling out everywhere.

"I HOPE HE WAS A GOOD BOY," Sora said, speaking to me like I was deaf. "THANK YOU FOR LETTING HIM STAY HERE WHILE I DID MY EXAMS. MARAMING SALAMAT PO."

Turning to Monolith, she switched to English. "Okay, Monolith, it's time to go back home. Did you hear the news from your mama? We have a lot to do!"

I pointed at my calendar to say, *Please, I want him to stay. I'm having a party. It's for him. Please stay, please.* Sensing my distress, Monolith pressed himself closer to me, throwing his arm across my torso as he wailed.

"Don't hug Grandpa Bayani like that," she chided him. "His old bones are not strong like yours. He's not a good playmate for you. We have to go."

Monolith sobbed as he latched onto me, and in return, I held him close, burying my face into his curly hair.

But in the end, she lured him away by dangling his most important possession in her hands.

"Monolith, look, I have your iPad. Don't you want to watch *Paw Patrol*, *Bubble Guppies*, *Peppa Pig*? If you don't come with me, your friends will miss you! Let's go home where you can play with them!" Dangling the glowing screen in the air, she quickly walked out of my room.

Monolith let my hand go limp and ran to her side, whining at the top of his lungs.

"Did you teach Grandpa Bayani any English?" she asked, closing the door behind them.

* * *

Hindi kita malimot	*I cannot forget you*
Ala-ala kita	*You are in my mind*
Hindi kita malimot	*I cannot forget you*
Minamahal kita	*Because I love you*

—HINDI KITA MALIMOT

After my family leaves for the resort, I fall back onto my pillows and rest. When I wake up, Rolly is sitting at the edge of my bed.

"Pa, can you come here?" he calls into the hallway. "I need you to bring me the Vicks. His breathing sounds a little stuffed up, so I'm going to rub it on his feet and put some socks on him. Thank you, Pa!"

My heavy eyelids flutter open, but Rolly isn't speaking to me; he's speaking to someone else he calls Pa. My senses sharpen as I jealously scan the room for another man.

Philippa pokes her head into the room, and immediately, I can see both of her parents in her. She has Rebekah's height and soft hair and dark skin, and Rolly's kind brown eyes and ready smile.

"Already got it," she says, tossing the jar to her father. "See, aren't you glad that I didn't go to the resort? What would you do without me?" She tilts her head in my direction. "Look, he's awake."

Rolly drops the Vicks and reaches for me with both hands.

"Tatay? Kilala niyo ba ako? Do you know who I am?"

I nod slowly, holding my breath so that I don't cry.

Rolly, the one who once filled the house with his songs and stories and laughter, is suddenly speechless.

"I just want to say—what I'm trying to say—I just—" Rolly bursts into tears, kneeling on the floor so he can see me eye-to-eye. "Pasensiya na po—I'm sorry that it took me this long to come. I never had enough time or enough money. Since she was a little girl, Philippa has been telling me that she wanted to come here and I kept promising her we would, but it's so hard to save money in Canada and time kept slipping away. Oh Tatay, if I only knew you were like this—"

I put my hand on top of his and squeeze, making him cry harder.

"Rebekah always wanted me to get out of care work and go back to university so I could get a better job, but I just couldn't do it. I love caregiving and I'm good at it. When I first started, her mother said that I'd always be in demand because it's so hard to find male caregivers, and she was right. So many people depend on me." He choked back a sob. "I know I shouldn't have left you the way I did, but I didn't think I had a choice. I could see my future with Rebekah and I needed to be with her. I never dreamed it meant that I wouldn't see you for seventeen years! I've thought of you every single day. Please, I know I don't deserve this from you, but please, please—forgive me."

I open my mouth and try to croak, "No, please forgive *me*," but the words only come out in a groan.

"Tatay, what are you trying to say?" Rolly asks, gesturing for Philippa to join him at my bedside.

My heart knows what it wants to say but my body won't cooperate. But there is one sound I *can* make. Looking straight into my granddaughter's eyes, I say it with all of the feeling in my heart: "Pa."

"He said my nickname!" Philippa exclaims, her smile lighting up the room. "Lolo Bayani knows who I am!"

"Pa! Pa! Pa!" I say over and over, my trembling hand on her cheek.

Rolly throws his arms around me and together, we finally complete the full arc of the kundiman: heartache and longing that finally gives way to happiness, fulfillment, and true love.

* * *

That night, the rest of the family returns from the resort smelling like sun, sweat, and chlorine.

"So how was your day?" Britney asks, making a face at Philippa. "Boring?"

"Pretty good, actually," she replies lightly.

Tering and Rolly spent the afternoon deciphering the old family recipe cards to present us with a feast of Batangas specialties: hearty kalderetang kambing with juicy pieces of goat, savoury bulalo stew slow-cooked for hours, crispy tawilis sardines from Lake Taal, and a big bowl of lomi with the perfect amount of cassava starch to make an exquisite sauce for the fresh noodles, with a bowl of fresh calamansi to make the flavours bright. And because no meal is complete without rice, Philippa asked me if she could make her grandmother's famous Jamaican rice and peas, and I readily agreed, making Rolly burst into tears all over again.

In the cool night breeze, the delectable fragrances spread throughout the house, making everyone eager to sit at our ancestral table that hasn't been used for so long.

Slowly, I come out of my room wearing my barong Tagalog and sit at the head of the table, studying each of my teenage grandchildren. They should be strangers to me, but in each of them, I can see traces of our ancestors whose portraits look down at us with pride.

"As you all know, this reunion has been a long time coming," Rolly says. "I'm happy that it's finally happened, and I know that Tatay is, too. So before we eat this incredible birthday feast, I think we need to sing a special song."

"Not the birthday song," Clark groans. "Anything but that!"

"Are you one? Are you two? Are you three?" Kent begins. "Guys, this'll take all night!"

Laughing heartily, Rolly turns to his daughter. "Philippa, will you do the honours?"

I hold my breath as she walks over to Inay's piano, but I'm sorely disappointed when she leaves the lid down and the sheet music untouched. But my disappointment gives way to shock as she picks up Tatay's bandurria, holding it in her slender arms and tuning the fourteen strings with ease.

She strums the first notes of "Bayan Ko" as Rolly gets up to sing. As the most revered of all of the kundiman, this is the unofficial Philippine anthem, and the most important love song for the Filipino people.

Rolly remembered.

And not only did he remember but, more importantly, he passed it down.

When the music begins, I close my eyes and make one birthday wish: that wherever he is, Monolith can dream of this tonight.

And as my heart fills with pride, I watch as my half-Jamaican, half-Filipino granddaughter channels the generations of ancestors who came before her, completely at home in the legacy that has been hers to inherit all along.

Pilipinas kong minumutya	*Philippines, my beloved*
Pugad ng luha ko at dalita	*Nest of tears and suffering*
Aking adhika	*My wish for you*
Makita kang	*Is to set you*
Sakdal laya!	*Completely free!*

—BAYAN KO

CHAPTER EIGHT

Little Manila Mumshie

I KNOW IT'S STRANGE for a fifteen-year-old to say this, but my mama is my best friend. She gave me everything I like about myself: my shiny, wavy hair, my amazing eyebrows, my perfectly heart-shaped face. With her smooth skin, bright smile, and fantastic clothes, she looks so young that she could be mistaken for my sister.

I love her so much that I don't even call her "Mama"—to me, she's "Mumshie."

She left me and Pa behind six years ago, but she always made sure that she was still part of our lives. Even after she went to Canada, every Sunday, she'd FaceTime us at exactly 7:30 a.m. so we could eat breakfast while she had dinner. We'd prop the phone up in her empty chair and talk to her like she was really beside us.

In between calls, she texted us constantly, celebrating everything from Pa launching his latest tourism campaign for the San Marco del Mudo Museum, to me scoring the starring role of the Singkil prince in the town dance troupe.

Mumshie loved sending us pictures with her friends in Toronto's Little Manila neighbourhood. Every time they picnicked by the José Rizal bust at Earl Bales Park, ate big kamayan feasts at Kabalen, or watched live OPM bands in the street during the Taste of Manila festival, Pa and I felt like we were part of the fun, too.

My favourite pictures were from the "weekender apartment" where Mumshie and her barkada of five best friends lived together from Friday night to Sunday night. Pooling their wages together, they rented the two-bedroom apartment, where they could sing karaoke, joke around, and relax after five days of caregiver work. Mumshie loved showing us the food they made, representing parts of the Philippines that we'd never been to—from the palapa-spiced chicken piaparan of the Maranao, to the bright coconut vinegar and calamansi-marinated fish kinilaw of the Visayas, to the crispy shrimp okoy dipped in the sukang Iloko of the Cordilleras. Mumshie's life looked like so much fun, and Pa and I couldn't wait for the day when we could finally join her in Toronto.

*   *   *

But on the March morning that Pa and I were finally supposed to join Mumshie in Canada, he came out of his bedroom, squeezed my shoulder, and said five words I will never forget: "Tell her I'm not coming."

He picked up his old leather briefcase and left for the museum like it was any other weekday. I was so shocked that I couldn't even call out to him. Pa had spoken with such seriousness, and yet, I didn't believe him until I ran to his room and threw open his suitcases, only to find that they were all empty.

I collapsed onto the floor, my chest heaving so hard that I could barely breathe.

Pa's sister, Tita Marki, arrived to drive us to the airport.

"He's—he's not—" I couldn't bring myself to say it, but I didn't have to.

As I tried to catch my breath, she handed me a folder of papers and said, "He told me to give this to you."

With shaking hands, I saw that Pa had signed the documents allowing me to emigrate on my own, and he had forged Mumshie's signature on every page.

"But he has to come with me. I need him—Mumshie needs him!"

"Jermayne, it's time to go," Tita Marki said, tucking the documents into my big purple backpack. "I can't let you miss your flight."

"But I can't go to Canada without Pa!"

"You can and you will," she said, leading me towards the car.

As she drove, I turned around in my seat and watched my little town fade away. On one side of San Marco, there were the rolling hills of the coffee farms, and on the other side of town, the historical plaza was proudly perched high on the green cliffs of the Tagaytay Ridge, with the river sparkling below. At the edge of the plaza, I spotted the big wooden doors of the museum. Pa was probably in his office, leisurely sipping kapeng barako and planning his next stupid museum exhibit, not even caring that I was about to go on the scariest journey of my life, possibly never to come back again.

Turning to face the rising sun over the yellow rocks of Mount Batulao, I clutched my plane ticket in my clammy hands.

At our despedida party, Pa had called it the golden ticket. Every person who came to say goodbye told us how lucky we were. Canada was the ultimate destination—a peaceful, rich country with free public education, free health care, and the freedom to pursue your dreams.

Everyone we knew told us how they thought of Canada as the promised land.

But if that was true, why didn't Pa come with me?

* * *

I spent most of the fourteen hours, forty-four minutes, and forty-four seconds on the direct flight to Toronto nervously pacing the narrow plane aisles, vomiting in the cramped toilet, and crying as I watched my reflection in the foggy plane window. Whenever I managed to drift off to sleep, I'd wake up to the flight attendants serving food, but I could barely eat with all of the anxiety, excitement, and despair rolling around in my stomach. At the Toronto airport, I rushed down the arrivals ramp and straight into Mumshie's open arms.

"Pa's not here," I said, my voice breaking. "He didn't come with me—I don't know what happened—I'm—I'm—"

Mumshie kissed my damp cheeks and held me tight.

"I know, Utoy," she said, using my childhood nickname to make me feel better. "What matters is that you're here now. Let's go home."

Her face was frozen into a forced smile. I knew she wasn't surprised because Tita Marki had already told her the news, but it still felt horrible.

Mumshie had been living in the attic of her employers' big house, but when Pa and I were about to arrive, she decided to move into the weekender apartment for good. On weekends, we would host her five best friends, but on weekdays, the apartment would be just for us.

It was incredible to finally step into a place that I had seen so many times before. It all felt so familiar: the turquoise-coloured couches, soft yellow blankets, gauzy white curtains, long wooden dining table, and the big TV and speakers, complete with karaoke microphones in a basket woven into the shape of a heart. It was even better than I'd dreamed it would be.

Flinging myself onto a smooth, velvety armchair, I called out, "Mumshie, I can't believe I'm actually here!"

She grinned. "I'm glad you're happy, Utoy. Now go take off your travelling clothes and change into your pambahay before we eat. You can change in our room."

"Our" room? I thought.

I passed an open bedroom with two mattresses crammed side by side, with everyone's things in neat piles at the foot of the beds. "Are we going to fit in here?"

Mumshie kissed my cheek. "Not this room—the girls agreed that since it's just you and me, the room next door is all ours."

Rushing into the second bedroom, I found a narrow, cozy space with a set of wooden bunk beds that had been painted yellow and white.

"It's so cute!" I exclaimed. "Like sleeping in a playground!"

I climbed up to the top bunk, where I had a view of the Sea-Hi Famous Chinese Food restaurant across the street, the red neon sign casting a warm glow into the room.

On the other side of the restaurant, there were streets filled with big, fancy houses as far as I could see. In our video calls, Mumshie used to point the camera outside to show us the neighbourhood where she worked, and it was incredible to see it in person. Their garages alone were larger than the cramped studio where my entire dance troupe rehearsed, and the yards were filled with trees that were covered in a perfect layer of white. The chimneys puffed curls of white smoke that blended into the clouds. With the falling snow, it looked like I had landed in the middle of a Christmas movie in March. I couldn't believe that from now on, this would be my home. I took out my phone and texted Pa.

> **Jermayne:** Made it to Canada! It's even better than I thought it would be! You'd love it here! Please try to come on the next flight!

"Ano gaaa, what's taking you so long?" Mumshie asked playfully, poking her head into our room, her shiny ponytail swishing against the doorframe.

"I'm just texting Pa," I replied.

"What did you tell him?" she asked, peeking at my phone.

After reading my text, she paused, choosing her words carefully.

"Utoy, if he didn't come today, I don't think he'll be coming anytime soon." The smile dropped from her face, making her suddenly look older. "I think it's best that we just move on."

* * *

That night, I lay in the bunk bed above Mumshie. The streetlamp cast a spotlight on the back of our door, where she'd hung my new school uniform. I wouldn't be going to a private school like I did back home, but because I was going to Catholic school, I still had to wear a uniform. She'd wanted me to start before March Break, but I'd begged her to give me some time to adjust.

"I remember how hard getting settled was for me with the jet lag, the cold weather, and the culture shock," she'd said, squeezing my hand. "Take all the time you need."

But she didn't know the real reason why I needed more time.

Looking at the sombre black uniform sweater, black pants, and black polo shirt, it looked like I was dressing for a funeral. I felt my anxiety levels rising.

"Mumshie, there's something I have to tell you," I said quietly. "I know why Pa didn't come with me. I'm not the kind of son he wants."

"What do you mean?" she asked, her sweet voice rising from the bunk below. "You're handsome and smart and so talented. You're the best son we could've ever asked for!"

"But that's the thing," I said slowly, my eyes focusing on the heavy black uniform pants. "I'm not just your son. Sometimes, I feel like a boy, and other times, I feel like something else. Not a girl, either. But—something more than that. Something in between."

For a full minute, she said nothing, the silence making it hard to breathe.

"I've called you every single Sunday for the past six years but you couldn't tell me this until now?" she finally asked, her voice strained.

"Mumshie, you and I are best friends. Are you honestly surprised?"

I squeezed my eyes shut until I heard her sigh. "No, I guess I'm not."

Taking a deep breath, I voiced the question I'd been waiting to ask her in person for the longest time: "Mumshie, will you still love me even though I'm like this?"

There was another long pause as she chose her words carefully. "I've waited for you for so long, to share my life abroad with you, to be in the same home as you, to breathe the same air as you. Do you know how long I've dreamed about being able to talk to you like this?"

Mumshie sat up, making our bunk bed shake, reaching up her hand to hold mine. "You are not a boy, and you are not a girl, and you know what else you are not? You are not a disappointment. I will love you no matter what."

"So, you're not mad? Promise?"

"Nothing you do could ever make me mad at you, Utoy," she said, squeezing my fingers. "Now what can I do to help you find out more about who you are?"

"Well, I wish you wouldn't call me 'Utoy' anymore. That's a nickname for little boys."

"Okay, Jermayne—do you still like that name? If you want me to call you something else, I will."

"No, it's the best name!" I cried. I hung over the side of our bunk bed, taking in her tear-stained, heart-shaped face that looked so much like mine. "Hey Mumshie, when you and Pa chose my name, did you realize that my spelling of 'Jermayne' could be for anybody—boys, girls, anyone? Did you spell it with a 'y' because you knew I'd turn out like this and one day, it would be perfect for me?"

"Ohh Jermayne, I love you so much!" Her fingers playfully poked and prodded the bottom of my mattress, making me laugh. "Now go to sleep!"

I wanted to rest, but there was one more thing I had to say. "Mumshie, I think I know why Pa didn't come."

"You do?"

"Last month, there was a costume contest at school, and we had to dress up as national heroes. I told Pa that I wanted to be Doña Gliceria because most people forgot that she was a heroine for giving her house, her ship, and her riches to the insurrectos and becoming the godmother of the revolution, right?"

I squeezed my eyes shut, but the tears still came.

"I begged Pa to let me borrow a costume from the museum, but the night before the contest, he just handed me a simple beige skirt. I went to my room and twirled in front of the mirror to see how it moved. When Pa walked in on me dancing, he gave me an old blanket and told me to wrap it around my legs. 'If you want to wear a skirt, go ahead,' he said. 'But if you do, you have to sit down on a chair and use this blanket to cover it. Now you're the sublime paralytic, Apolinario Mabini.' I told him that this wasn't the hero I wanted to be, but he just said, 'You're a boy from Batangas. This is the hero you *should* be.'

"The next day, he caught me walking to school wearing the skirt. He got out of his car, tied the blanket around my waist with a hard knot, and drove me to the contest, where he stayed just to watch me sit in a chair and do nothing.

"Ever since then, he's said less and less to me. That was even worse than him yelling. I think that's why he didn't come to Canada. If I'd known, I would've just been Mabini from the beginning. I'm sorry, Mumshie. I messed everything up."

"Let's not worry about your pa," she said. "Try to see it this way: now that he's not here, you have the freedom to be the person you want to be. You're in a new country and nobody knows you but me, and I'll support you no matter what. You don't even have to go to Catholic school. After March Break, I can sign you up for public school so you can wear whatever makes you happy, no more uniform. How does that sound?"

"I think I need time to figure out who I am so that when people meet me for the first time, they'll be meeting the real me," I said. "That'll make me really happy. And after I start school, we can video call Pa and he'll see how well I'm doing here, and then, maybe he'll come to be with us!"

"Maybe," Mumshie said, her voice sounding small in the dark.

*   *   *

In the morning, Mumshie returned the uniform. With the black clothes gone, I knew that I could be anyone I wanted to be, but the possibilities were overwhelming. I wanted to be barefaced, but I also wanted statement eyes and gorgeous red lips. I wanted to cut my hair short, but I also wanted to grow it long enough for a beautiful balayage braid. I wanted to clip my nails, but I also wanted long acrylics with metallic ruby polish studded with rhinestones. I decided that until I figured out the new person I would be, I would stay as invisible as I could. No going out for walks along Bathurst Street, no talking to the neighbours, no posts on any socials. I needed to stay home and think.

I remembered the times when members of my dance troupe would bother me with stupid interrogations about celebrity love teams.

"Do you like Dingdong Dantes or Marian Rivera?"

"What are you talking about?" I'd ask, rolling my eyes.

"KathNiel, JaDine, LizQuen, AlDub—tell us, do you like the boys or the girls?" they'd demand, crowding around me so I couldn't get away.

"No to all of them, yes to all of them," I'd reply, trying to sound casual.

"You can't have it both ways! You have to pick!"

"I'm too busy for this!" I'd snap, going to my safe space onstage where I could rehearse my moves alone.

But in Canada, anything was possible. When I was alone in the apartment, I performed the folk dances I loved, dismissing the male steps that I'd already mastered. I tried out the female parts that I'd committed to memory, delighted at how naturally my old partners' moves came to me.

I chose the dances based on items I found in the room where Mumshie's friends left their belongings in little piles at the foot of their beds. First, there was the thick yellow bandana that made me think of a beak. Inspired, I tied it on like a hairband and pivoted around the apartment, flapping my arms rhythmically, dancing Itik-Itik as if I'd been doing it my whole life. Admiring myself in the reflection in the window, I realized with joy that I'd transformed into a glorious, graceful bird.

Then, I found a sparkly, sheer periwinkle shawl to wrap around my shoulders. Grabbing the palm leaf fan that hung by the fire alarm, I whirled around the room and fanned myself flirtatiously at my invisible suitor, spinning to the Cariñosa music in my head.

But when I discovered a scrunchie with little bells, I knew I had the perfect accessory to try one more dance. Grabbing four scarves and rolling them into long lines, I criss-crossed them in the centre of the living room. When I put the scrunchie around my ankle, I instantly transformed into a proud Singkil princess. I jutted my chin upwards and stamped my foot, letting the bells jingle deliciously in the expectant air.

Imagining the scarves transforming into clapping bamboo sticks, I heard the familiar *boom-boom-boom, clap-clap* rhythm in my head and stepped into the middle of the quaking bamboo forest. As I imagined my handsome prince arriving—to admire me, to protect me, to fall in love with me—I twirled my fans in the air with all the allure, poise, and bravery of an esteemed Maranao princess.

I caught my reflection in the window. It looked like I was dancing on top of the Sea-Hi Famous Chinese Food restaurant, the bright red letters acting as my stage, and I was filled with embarrassment.

"This is who you're going to be in Canada?" I heard Pa shouting in my head. "This is why I didn't want to come with you!"

It wasn't that I actually wanted to be the princess—somehow, I wanted to be both prince and princess combined. It suddenly seemed so stupid.

For the millionth time, I reminded myself that Pa didn't hate gay people. In San Marco, there were a few older gay men who hung out outside of the beauty salon, and whenever we passed by, he smiled as they screamed Celine Dion's "It's All Coming Back to Me Now" into a screechy microphone or playfully jostled each other to ask him who had the best otso-otso dance moves. He never said anything rude about them, never even gave them a disparaging glance.

And he was never rude to Tita Marki, with her low voice, spiky hair, loose T-shirts and jeans, and, of course, her general distaste for anything feminine. We never saw her with a partner, but Pa once casually told me that if his sister ever brought someone home to meet us, it probably wouldn't be a man.

In Singkil, Tita Marki would never want to be the princess or the prince. She would be content to kneel down, eyes to the ground as she dutifully clapped the bamboo sticks, making herself indispensable and yet completely unmemorable to the audience.

That wasn't me at all. More than anything, I wanted to be the star. I just didn't know which role I wanted to be in when I stepped into the spotlight.

*   *   *

On Friday night, Mumshie's barkada came over for the weekend, a commotion of imitation Louis Vuitton purses and JanSport backpacks and black puffer jackets pouring out of the rickety elevator. They all had glossy hair, smooth skin, and fresh lipstick in shades ranging from crimson red to coral pink. As they showered me with hugs and kisses, the attention was so overwhelming that it felt like the five of them had merged into one person.

"Hey, it's the dance star of San Marco del Mudo!"

"Look at that face—just like Maricar's!"

"You must be so happy to be with your 'Mumshie'! Ang kyuuut!"

Mumshie came and proudly patted my shoulders. "Isn't Jermayne so good-looking?" she asked.

"So pogi!"

"Gwapong gwapo talaga!"

"Yes, he's growing up to be such a handsome man!"

Everyone beamed at me but I stepped back, upset.

"What's wrong?" one of them asked, poking me in the ribs. "Jermayne doesn't think he's good-looking?"

"Bakit, shy ba siya?"

"So modest!"

"No, it's just..." Mumshie's voice trailed off.

Silently, she looked at me, eyebrows raised, as if to ask, *Do you want to explain who you are to them?*

And I looked away to reply, *No thank you, I'm not ready yet.*

Mumshie stood between us, jokingly spreading her arms like she was a bodyguard. "Hoy, tumahimik kayo, you're scaring my bedspacer!"

One of her friends bumped her away with her hip and put her hand on my arm. "Are we overwhelming you, baby? Sorry, ha—it's just that all of us miss our families and you're the first one here!"

Another one pulled me close and sniffed my cheek. "You still smell like home! Ang sarap! Relax ka muna, okay? Let us make a welcome-to-Canada dinner for you!"

Mumshie's friends crammed into the tiny kitchen, expertly manoeuvring around each other as they prepared their dishes.

"So, how was your week, everybody?" Mumshie called out.

The question sparked a series of rants about their employers' children.

"This morning, Llewellyn and Bronwyn said that they won't bathe anymore—they even threw their expensive soap into the garbage. That Aēsop stuff is sixty dollars a bottle, you know! My parents would have put me up for adoption if I did that!"

"Ayyy sis, you want to talk about wasting expensive stuff? Elliott is teething, so his parents asked me to wear one of those fifty-dollar organic rubber necklaces so that he can chew it whenever I hold him. I think it's so gross, walking around covered in his laway! I put the necklace away, but then I found him chewing on the dog's squeaky toys. When I told him to make better choices, he decided to go straight to the source: he bit the beagle's ear! Grabe, they both howled—putaragis, ang sakit sa tenga!"

"These Canadian kids talaga," Mumshie said, laughing hard. "But you know, their parents are something else, too, jusko po! My employers just asked me to spend the entire March Break with them at their chalet in Mont-Tremblant. It sounds fancy-fancy but we all know what this really means: 'Maricar, we'll be spending our entire vacation on the ski slopes, so we need you to watch the baby!'"

Everyone grumbled knowingly.

"Parehas kami, Maricar. I'm spending March Break on a Norwegian cruise, and my employers got adjoining oceanview rooms. You know what that means, girls: the parents will get their own room, while I have to stay in the floating prison next door with the kids. The only way that I'll get to have a break from them is if I throw myself overboard!"

"At least you're on a cruise! I'll be spending March Break with my employers at their new villa in Italy. It's such an old house that I already know what's going to happen. If they see any bugs, they're going to make me kill them. 'You're used to them because you grew up with flying cockroaches, right?' they'll ask. I'm going to be brought all the way to Italy just to be their in-house exterminator! Nakakaloka, ayaw ko!"

"Mine are making me come to a resort in the Caribbean. Grabe! You know how it'll be—the parents will stay inside, getting massages and taking naps and drinking margaritas, and they'll tell me to bring the kids outside to play in the pool. But since kids aren't allowed in the pool without an adult, I told them that I don't know how to swim. So instead of saying that they would play with their own kids, my employers made me take private swimming lessons all week! Does this mean that if the kids drown abroad, it'll be my fault? Por Diyos por santo!"

"For caregivers, it's inevitable," Mumshie sighed. "Right when you think they'll give you a break, they make you work some more!"

I pulled her close. "Mumshie, are you serious?" I asked, my voice low. "You're really leaving me alone for a whole week?"

She put her hand on my cheek. "All of us have to go, Jermayne. Plus, I can't say no when my employers helped bring you here. They've been so good to me and I owe them so much. You're fifteen now, and you managed to come here all by yourself. You'll be fine on your own for a week, no?"

"I guess," I replied, my stomach churning.

Mumshie's friends placed their food in the middle of the table. My mouth watered as I finally smelled the special dishes that I'd only seen in pictures: the Maranao palapa-spiced chicken piaparan; the creamy, tangy Visayan kinilaw; and the Igorot-style crispy shrimp okoy complete with sukang Iloko. As I was about to fill up my plate, Mumshie cleared her throat.

"Dear Lord, thank you for bringing Jermayne here," she prayed aloud as everyone closed their eyes. "This is the fulfillment of all of my hard work and sacrifices. As we pray that all of our families will be reunited with us someday, we also pray that you'll make Jermayne happy with us in Canada!"

"Amen!" they cried.

Hurriedly making the sign of the cross, I filled my mouth with so much food that nobody could ask me to talk.

*   *   *

By one-thirty in the morning, Mumshie's friends' voices were hoarse from all of the karaoke, teasing, and giggling. Three of them went to their shared bedroom, and the other two converted the couch into a double bed.

As I settled into my comforter, I heard them calling out to one another.

"Did anyone see my scrunchie? The one with the bells?"

"Ayy, you always lose your things!"

"I swear, I always leave it on my bed with my bandana."

"I think it's here in the couch cushions!"

"How did it get there?"

"Did anyone see my shawl?"

"Whose scarf is on my bed?"

"That's mine! Is this one yours?"

"How did they get mixed up?"

"I don't know!"

Mumshie cleared her throat, but I just smiled to myself in the dark.

* * *

I didn't sleep for long. Mumshie's friends had all gathered in the room next door, and I could hear them through the thin walls.

"Girls, did Maricar tell you what Gerald did to her and Jermayne?"

"It's so sad. Such a selfish man to abandon them like that!"

"Another broken family! Why does our group have such bad luck with men?"

"Ehh, she doesn't seem too upset about it. Maybe it's because we all know how normal this is."

"Remember when my husband stopped talking to me the minute I told him I got the papers to bring him here? Thirty years old and he still didn't want to leave his mommy. Blocked me on Instagram, Facebook, everything!"

"And what about my husband? You remember how he started a whole shadow family while I was gone? Last night, he called to tell me he wasn't cheating on me—he just needed servicing, like a car. I told him that he could drive his car into a ditch!"

"I thought I was lucky with my Rommel, but yesterday, he texted me and said, 'I'll come to Canada with the children, but you have to release me upon arrival. I want to go and live with my tito in Labrador.' Susmaryosep, Labrador? Release upon arrival? Is that what I worked so hard for? For him to run off to the edge of Canada and just leave me here alone?"

"Inday, I still think you should tell him no."

"You know I can't."

"Why?"

"Same reason why Maricar tried so hard to make her marriage work. I love him too much!"

"Poor girl."

"Oo nga, kawawa si Maricar."

"Is that why Jermayne is too shy to talk to us?"

"Maybe he's in shock."

"You can't expect a boy that young to be okay without his Pa."

"Why not? He's fifteen—not much younger than we were when we all left our families. We were just twenty-three, twenty-four! We all turned out okay, didn't we?"

They murmured in agreement and their voices faded away as I drifted off to sleep.

* * *

In my dream, I was at the San Marco del Mudo fiesta, and about to perform the finale of Sayaw sa Bangko. The town plaza was bathed in a warm, twilight glow, and the audience was captivated as the music grew to a dramatic swell. Smiling confidently at the crowd, I approached the pyramid of wooden benches, the spotlight following me the whole way as I expertly jumped higher and higher, reaching the fifth level as everyone held their breath. At the top, there was a pretty girl waiting for me. I took my dance partner by the waist and gently twirled her around, her checkered skirt catching beautifully in the breeze.

"Ready for the big finale?" she asked. Before I could reply, she let go of my hand and gracefully hopped to the ground below, bowing to raucous applause.

She's not supposed to bow without me! I thought, rubbing my sweaty hands on my cuffed short pants. I scowled down at her but the music was abruptly cut and she disappeared. The hundreds of tiny maya birds who settled on the electrical wires every night began to panic, swarming into a huge black cloud around me and flying out to Mount Batulao—a sign that made my stomach drop.

Suddenly, the stage below me lurched forward and my pyramid of benches was transported to the opposite end of the plaza, right to the edge of San Marco's sheer cliffs, where the river angrily rushed below.

"What's going on? Get me down!" I screamed.

Up from the mist, a new partner jumped to the top of the benches with a grand flourish.

It was me, but with bold ruby lips, wavy raven hair, smokey eyes, and a fiery red sequinned skirt that gleamed in the spotlights.

As I reached out to grasp my partner's waiting hands, I watched in horror as the river swirled up the cliffs and collided with the darkening sky, swiftly transforming into a howling typhoon. The storm began to circle the town plaza, the angry winds screaming as they closed in on the stage, ripping up the stairs one by one.

Oblivious to the storm, the audience watched us raptly, completely focused on the finale of Sayaw sa Bangko. They were pointing at me, jeering at how scared I was.

I spotted Pa standing at the back of the crowd, arms crossed impatiently, impervious to the trees and tin roofs that were flying right behind me.

"Pa, come help me! Please!" I yelled over the howling gale.

He caught the eye of my partner, whose red lips pursed together, pointing down.

Pa nodded approvingly.

Lip curling up into a sneer, my partner shoved me off the benches and I plummeted straight into the deafening winds, past the jagged cliffs and into the roaring abyss below.

The last thing I saw was a flash of the red sequinned skirt triumphantly lit up in spotlights.

I woke up in a cold sweat, knowing one thing: I had to become that other version of myself before it killed me.

* * *

On Saturday night, as I lay in my bunk bed after dinner, I heard Mumshie's friends bickering as they tried to make plans.

"I want to go to Marcelina's!"

"Another karaoke night? I'm tired of hearing all of you sing!"

"You're just mad because you never get the high score."

"The machine is broken! It doesn't like my Ilocano accent."

"Ha! Too scared to compete against a Sugbuanon, is that it?"

"How about we just get peach mango pies at Jollibee?"

"That's too far to walk!"

"We could take the bus."

"That's too close to pay for the bus!"

"How about Maharlika?" Mumshie asked, her voice smoothly cutting through the bickering. "Our favourite performer's on tonight!"

"Eeek! That's perfect!"

Her friends excitedly started to get ready, going through piles of clothes, searching for something cute to wear.

Mumshie came into our room, propping her slender chin up on my bunk bed railing.

"Jermayne, you'll come with us, right? I know you're too young for a bar, but tonight's headliner knows us. They'll let you in."

I shrugged. "If you want me to come, then sure, I guess."

With a smile, she opened her closet wide. "Whatever you want to wear is yours tonight. I just want you to be happy."

Eagerly jumping down from my bunk bed, my hands flew through her wardrobe until I found the perfect outfit: a tight little black sequinned dress with a high slit in the thigh.

"That's my favourite, too!" she said. "But it's not the right one for you."

I sat down on her bed, hurt. "But I thought you said—"

"Si Jermayne naman!" she said, grinning. "I have the same dress in red, and I think it'd look even better on you." She took it out of the closet, holding it up to me, the red fabric of my dreams lighting up the room.

"What will your friends think?" I asked, running my hands across the material.

"They'll think you look amazing."

I paused. "Are you sure you're okay with me going out like this?" I asked cautiously.

Mumshie kissed my head. "If it makes you happy, I'm happy," she said.

*   *   *

At Maharlika, Mumshie and her friends descended upon the table closest to the stage and started to settle in, happily showing off their strapless dresses, slinky bakuna blouses, and tight black pleather leggings as they shed their heavy winter coats.

There were only a handful of customers. By the bar, there was a bald man and his young Pinay girlfriend who giggled drunkenly as her fake eyelash fell into her cocktail. In the back, beside a mural of a farmer riding a blue carabao in front of the CN Tower, a group of students wearing Seneca College sweatshirts messily poured a pitcher of beer, roaring with laughter as it dripped onto the sticky floor.

I noticed that the tables and chairs Mumshie had picked were the exact same bright red as my dress. Despite my amazing outfit, I kept my big black coat on, not ready to reveal my new look just yet.

As the snow started to fall, I gazed out of the window at Little Manila. Mumshie had sent us so many photos of her life in Canada, but I noticed that she didn't send everything. She told me that she lived in "Little Manila," so I was expecting a mall, a fancy hotel, a plaza with street food vendors, a cathedral. Instead, it was just a quiet neighbourhood of hair salons, bakeries, remittance offices, abandoned storefronts and turo-turo restaurants. The squat brick buildings looked like they had been designed by people who had failed architecture school. The neighbourhood was nothing like I'd expected.

As Mumshie and her friends burst out laughing, their tipsy shrieks piercing the loud pop music, I realized that Pa wouldn't have fit in here at all. Not just in Little Manila, but in Mumshie's Toronto world. He wouldn't have wanted to host sleepovers every weekend. He wouldn't have wanted to hang out with Mumshie's girlfriends at a bar like this.

Pa wasn't suited for this life at all.

And before she left us, I don't think that Mumshie was, either.

I realized this was the Canadian version of Mumshie—that maybe back in San Marco, this was the person who had been inside of her all along, waiting to be reborn abroad. And because she had found her true self in Canada, she was happy to help me find myself, too.

"Ready for the show?" Mumshie called out, winking at me as the bar went dark and erupted into cheers.

Two spotlights illuminated the room and a disco ball cast glittery rainbows across the floor. When the doors to the stairwell slammed open, a dazzling drag queen emerged, strutting onto the stage with svelte brown arms in the air, clapping along to a Rihanna song. "Are you ready to feel like the only girl in the world?" the flirtatious voice called out.

I gasped at the lava-red body-hugging gown, the glossy wig with the cascading dark waves, and the shiny golden ear cuff with the three stars and the Philippine sun.

"It's Miss Universe!!!" everyone screamed.

"Oh no no," admonished the drag queen, wagging a glittery fake fingernail in the air. "You've heard of Catriona Gray? Well, I'm her upgraded version: *Riri Gay*!"

I felt a sense of impending doom as the drag queen strutted straight towards me. Lifting a long, hairless leg and hooking a white thigh-high platform boot onto the back of my chair, tipping me backwards so I was stuck in midair, Riri Gay called out, "And who's this little one in the big winter coat?"

"That's my baby!" Mumshie called out.

"Wow, so progressive, bringing your precious baby to my show!" Riri Gay blew Mumshie a kiss and she pretended to faint.

"Ask him to dance! He's a dancer!" her friends cried.

Riri Gay stood in front of me, dramatically extending a gorgeously manicured hand as the intro of "This Is What You Came For" filled the bar.

I shook my head again and again. "No, no, I can't."

"If you're a dancer, prove it onstage with me!"

"No thank you."

"Go have fun, Jermayne!" Mumshie said, urging me on.

The entire table started cheering: "Jer-mayne! Jer-mayne! Jer-mayne!"

Part of me longed to go up, but the other part of me just wanted to stay put. My dress was so similar to the drag queen's; it was absolutely embarrassing. Was this Mumshie's plan the whole time? Bring me to a drag show and hope I'd get inspired? I loved being in the spotlight, but the scuffed little stage at Maharlika was not the place for my big debut. It wasn't the right time, the right space, the right anything.

I didn't want to be disrespectful to Mumshie, so I pretended to laugh and playfully propelled Riri Gay back onto the stage. "This is your show," I exclaimed. "You're the one everyone came for!"

"I'll come back later tonight!" Riri Gay promised, sashaying away.

Leaning over to Mumshie, I said, "I'm so hot in here. I'm going outside to cool off."

"Why don't you take off your coat?"

"I just need some air. I'll be back in a minute."

As I slipped outside, I saw Riri Gay transform the bar into a Miss Universe runway, delivering Catriona Gray's stunning lava walk to Rihanna's rhythms in a perfect mash-up between beauty queen and pop diva that felt both inspirational and out of reach at the same time.

* * *

Even on a Saturday night, Little Manila was dead. As I walked, the only company I had were some cars and half-empty city buses driving by, their tires making a sloshing sound in the wet snow. Wandering over to the middle of an empty piece of land, I sighed as I noticed the sign: Bathurst-Wilson Parkette. Was this their town plaza? Even the Little Manila park was lacklustre. They couldn't have named it after a national hero, like Mabini, Rizal, Doña Gliceria, or Tandang Sora? I supposed it was just as well—it was just a few empty benches and some trellises made out of some damp wood. Not even a proper stage to dance on.

Scraping away the wet snow with my boots, I found a red sign embedded into the concrete: Mabuhay. This was a word used at formal events to welcome a crowd, but here, there was nothing welcoming at all.

It felt strange to admit because I'd waited for years to leave, but I suddenly missed home. I missed the warm sun, the green cliffs, the rushing river, the big stage in the town plaza, and even Pa's beloved museum. Toronto was my fresh start, but still—it was normal to feel homesick, wasn't it?

I reached for my phone and called Pa, but it went straight to voicemail.

"Hi Pa, I know it's like, ten in the morning back home, and that you're probably at church, but I just wanted to say hi. I'm walking around here in Little Manila, and, well, it's not what I expected. I'm going to be alright, but I wanted to say that I miss you. And you're not going to believe this, but I miss San Marco del Mudo, too! Anyway, can you call me back when you can? I really need to talk to you."

Shoving my phone back into my pocket, I blew on my fingers to keep them warm.

"Did you say San Marco del Mudo?"

I squinted into the dark and saw a slight woman coming towards me. As she approached, I noticed that her coat was worn, with dirty handprints all over the black fabric. Her lifeless hair poked out from beneath her hood. She stepped out of the shadows and stood below the streetlight, making it seem like the dark circles under her eyes took up half of her face. "Are you from San Marco del Mudo, Batangas?" she asked, her voice timid and hopeful.

"I just arrived," I replied cautiously.

"We're from there, too," she said. "We're new to Toronto, just like you."

"We?"

She gestured to the edge of the park that backed up against the overpass walls. I saw the silhouette of a little boy plunging his hands into a pile of ice shards and throwing them at a mural. The ice shattered against the concrete wall, leaving white blemishes all over the peaceful lakeside scene.

"That's Monolith," she said.

"Why is he out so late?"

She shrugged, jostling an Incredible Hulk backpack on her slender shoulders. "I was told that if he won't sleep, I should try taking him outside for some fresh air and exercise."

"At ten o'clock at night?"

She peered up at me, examining my face. "Are you related to Maricar? She went to my elementary school—she was a few years older than me. She tutored me in English. You look just like her."

I nodded, surprised. "That's my mother."

"She's here? Can you bring me to her?" she asked, her voice eager. "I need to speak to her!"

"Why?"

"It's been a long time, but she'll remember me, I just know it. I need to ask her something important!"

I stepped back, unsure.

"My employer is going to Blue Mountain for March Break and I have to go, too. They need me to take care of their children while they ski, but I don't know where to leave Monolith. Could Maricar take care of him?"

"Sorry, but she's going away with her own employers to Mont-Tremblant," I replied bitterly. "They're going on a ski trip, too."

"What about her friends? She was always so outgoing. Surely she has a big barkada."

"They're all going away with their employers, too."

"But you're staying behind?" she asked, coming closer to me. "How old are you? Fifteen? Sixteen? You'll be alone, too. You can keep each other company. Monolith has already been to two different children's centres, and they won't take him for overnight stays. My old friends in Oakville won't answer my calls anymore. No one can take him for a week. Except for you."

I glanced at the little boy as he made grunting noises in the snow, digging until he reached the mud, his mittens turning dark and damp.

"Since he doesn't speak, he's very quiet, see? He won't be a problem for you. Please help me. I don't know who else to ask."

"You don't even know me."

"I know your family. That's good enough."

On the other side of the intersection of Bathurst and Wilson, I heard Mumshie on Wilson Avenue, calling out my name. As I turned, the woman desperately reached out to me. My black coat fell open, exposing my red sequinned dress. I gasped and tried to hide it, but if she saw it, she didn't care.

"Please, please, can Monolith spend March Break with you?"

CHAPTER NINE

Monolith Speaks

HE COMES INTO THE APARTMENT like he's scared of me. Eyes big, eyebrows raised, mouth frozen in a fake friendly smile, hand moving in a stiff wave. Everyone looks like this when they meet me.

I'm not a monster, I want to tell him.

I'm Monolith.

I'm almost six years old.

I'm a boy.

Not a monster.

Mama quickly gives some instructions to him, but from the way he nervously glances around the apartment, I can tell that he isn't really listening. Mama kisses me goodbye and rushes out, pulling a suitcase behind her, leaving us all alone. She told me she had to go away, but for how long? It won't just be for a few hours. I'm smart. I know what suitcases mean. Suitcases mean that you will go far away, possibly to leave someone behind forever.

When I see that the stranger brought a big purple backpack, I'm immediately suspicious. Did Mama ask him to put me in that tight hugging jacket at bedtime, like Miss Magda and Mister Jan did in our old apartment? Did she say he could shove a camera in my face like Miss Forte and ask people to give him money? Did she tell him he could give me sleepytime pills like Kuya Paulo did? My eyebrows push together hard as I think. What's he going to do to me?

I need to find out what's in that backpack.

As he takes off his winter boots, I rip open the zipper to see what's inside.

"Stop that!" he shouts, tugging at his boot and losing his balance as he bumps his shoulder into the wall.

Ignoring him, I pull out everything in the bag.

There's a pink sweater, a red polka-dot skirt, and two glittery white pyjama shirts that are long enough to be dresses. Why would a boy have these things? Did he take a girl's backpack by accident?

As he takes off his puffy black coat, I see that he's wearing a sparkly sweater that hangs off of one shoulder. It's purple like ube.

I know what he's going to do to me.

He's going to make me into a girl.

I push the bag away and shriek. I wish I could run into my room and lock the door, but Mama moved us into a studio apartment. When she first told me about it, she tried to make it sound fancy, but now I know what "studio apartment" really means: no walls. Nowhere to hide.

The first time she took me here, I screamed and ran to every corner of the apartment, slamming my hands against the four corners to tell her that I hate places without bedroom doors and I hate places without locks that make a click-click sound, I hate it I hate it I hate it I hate it, but she just wouldn't listen.

When I finally emptied out all of the screams inside of me, she crouched down on the floor, her face to mine. "Monobaby, we're moving here to Toronto for my new caregiving job," she said, brushing the sweaty curls from my forehead. "It has better pay than the seniors home, so I'll be able to save up to get you the help you need before you start school. Give it a chance and you'll like it here. Promise."

But I won't give it a chance.

In a studio apartment, there's only one place to hide: the Comfort Room.

I run inside, slam the thin wooden door behind me, and let out a howl so loud that I hope Mama can hear. Where is she? When is she coming back? Why did she leave me? I'm tired of people leaving me!

I howl and howl, my voice bouncing off of the bathtub, the mirror, the walls with the chipped yellow paint. Doesn't Mama want me anymore?

This morning, Mama tried to tell me something, but her stream of English words was too fast. I pushed my face into the couch cushions and whined to tell her that I didn't understand, but then she left with a suitcase, so now I'm going to live in this Comfort Room forever and ever.

I chew on the edge of the orange bath mat until the little strings taste like blood.

"Monolith, let me explain why I'm here." The voice is soft and low on the other side of the door.

I hold my breath. What does this stranger want?

"For the next seven days, both our mamas will be staying with their employers for March Break. You and I are going to be together all week. We can keep each other company. I don't want you to be scared of me. I'm here to be your friend. Whenever you're ready, you can open the door. I'll be patient. Monolith, are you listening? Nakikinig ka ba?"

My ears perk up at the music of his words.

The familiar Tagalog sounds float beneath the door, filling my mind with happier days.

* * *

My earliest memories are of Tita Sora at her desk: messy ponytail, brown glasses, lips making whisper-noises as she read. Whether she was focused on a textbook, a laptop, or a stack of freshly printed papers, nothing could bother her—not even me yelling or turning our little shared bedroom upside-down.

If Tita Sora had a deadline to meet and had to concentrate extra hard, my Lola Tering would come over to cook and clean and play with me. Unlike Tita Sora's soft computer hands, Lola's ancient farmer hands felt hard at the fingertips. I loved to pretend to bite them as she crinkled her old face into a million lines and pretended to yelp in threes: "Aray-aray-aray!"

I thought we had so much fun together, but sometimes, before she left our house for her falling-down shack at the edge of the coffee plantations, Lola Tering would put her hand on Tita Sora's shoulder.

"Don't you think you should bring Monolith to a doctor?"

"There's nothing wrong with Monolith. He's just a little delayed. Boys are like that."

"We could go to an albularyo, a manghihilot, someone who can heal him and—"

"No thank you," Tita Sora interrupted, not looking up from her work. "I believe in science."

"You're an environmental scientist. You study the climate, not the brain. Why can't you just—"

"I don't believe in magic."

"It's not magic, these are our ancestors' ways of healing and—"

"It's the old way. Monolith doesn't need that."

"But—"

"No, Nanay. Ate Vera left me in charge of him. We're not talking about this again."

Lola Tering would throw up her worn old hands and walk down the dusty road to her home. As I watched her go, my heart would always fill up with love for Tita Sora. She made me feel perfect.

In our own little world, we were completely happy.

Until Pa came to live with us.

One rainy night, we were at the dinner table when a loud pounding on the door made me drop my fork, rice grains scattering everywhere.

"You know what a dropped fork means—we're about to be visited by a man," Tita Sora said lightly, trying to cover up the worried look on her face.

We opened the door and found Pa hunched over on the front step. With his arms open wide and his soaking wet sando and shorts and his puffy face, he was no man—he looked more like a scarecrow from my picture books.

He tried to hug me but I hid behind Tita Sora's legs.

"What are you doing here?" she asked.

"I need to live closer to my son," he begged. "Sora, please take pity on me. My parents are dead. My siblings moved far away. My wife abandoned me for another country. I'm all alone now. Monolith is all I have. He needs to know me. What's a boy without his pa?"

I pulled on Tita Sora's skirt and whined as loudly as I could. I didn't like his sour breath or his wet skin or his dirty fingernails or his wild red eyes. I thought she understood me, but instead of turning him away into the downpour, she gave him the spare bedroom.

"Monolith, you and I always sleep beside each other anyway," she said that night, running her long fingers through my hair to make me relax. "Naawa ako sa kanya." She pitied him so much that she couldn't say no.

Pa was just one person, but he took up so much space. His dusty tsinelas were scattered around the front door, his stinking cigarette butts piled up in rusted tin cans, his half-eaten food lay forgotten outside in the dirty kitchen where the cockroaches and maggots and ants and stray cats and dogs feasted on his scraps. He was everywhere.

Even the air was heavy with his angry words. It was always "Hayop kayo!" and "Lintek!" and "Tangina mo!" as he stumbled in the door late at night, toppling over yesterday's bottles of Fundador and Red Horse, leaving his sweaty sabongero clothes all over the furniture and slamming the door to his room. Sometimes we heard him throwing up in the kitchen sink and stumbling against the thin walls, but I was never scared. Whenever he came home, Tita Sora protected our room with a big click-click lock to keep us safe.

"When this door is locked up nice and tight, we can rest well and dream of better places," she said, holding me close, her nose in my hair.

Every night, when Tita Sora turned out the lights, I knew that as long as I heard the click-click, Pa couldn't bother us.

During the day, he slept soundly, too tired to care that we were even there.

As long as we didn't make any noise.

But one dark afternoon, when a super typhoon was coming, Tita Sora raced to finish something important on her computer before the brownouts began.

In the storm, Lola Tering wouldn't be coming to keep me occupied. With no one to play with me, I was so bored.

I snapped all of my crayons in half like the trees breaking outside. I built a tower out of our clothes and tore it apart like a house being destroyed in the angry winds. I made a pile of my stuffed toys and threw them around like people caught in a typhoon, bashing them against windows and walls and pretending to submerge them in our laundry basket like they were drowning. In our little room, I created my own super typhoon, but Tita Sora was so focused on her charts and graphs that she didn't notice a thing.

Rummaging through our closet, I discovered an old picture book. On the cover, there was a cartoon man and woman coming out of a big bamboo that had been broken in half. I pulled on Tita Sora's skirt and whined for her to read it to me.

"That's my old Malakas at Maganda book," she said, barely glancing from her glowing screen. "Monolith, Tita needs to work right now. With this storm, we might have a brownout soon, and I really need to submit this research paper. Just read to yourself, okay?"

I whined and whined to remind her that I didn't know how to read, but she ignored me.

Annoyed and grumpy, I crossed the house and pushed open Pa's door. He had just come home from a drinking session that lasted until the morning, and had fallen asleep on his little bed, the fan blowing cold air on his dirty, smelly feet.

I pulled on his arm once.

Twice.

Three times.

Four times.

On the fifth time, he opened one red eye and groaned.

"Ano ga? What do you want?" he asked, his breath sour with alcohol.

I eagerly thrust the book in front of him, showing him the magical picture of a serene couple climbing out of the bamboo, and whined for him to read it to me.

"Sora!" he yelled, squeezing his red eyes tight and aiming his words at the ceiling. "Why's this stupid boy bothering me? Sora!"

The growing typhoon winds drowned out his words.

"Walang galang sa matanda, eh? No respect! Sora, get him out of here! I'm warning you!"

Grabbing the book out of my hand, he rolled it up and smacked my face with it so hard that I fell backwards onto his grimy floor. An old staple caught on my cheek, slicing it open. I clutched my swelling cheek and began to cry.

"Tanga! Gago! Tarantado!" he shouted, calling me stupid in different ways. "You're the dumbest child on the planet! The least you can do is be quiet and let me forget that you exist!"

He reached out to grab me but I flung myself under his bed. I thought he would try to pull me out, but instead, he charged into Tita Sora's room.

She hadn't locked the click-click door.

"Sent!" she called out happily. "Monolith, I submitted my paper! Nasaan ka? Where are you?"

Pa threw the book at her laptop, toppling it to the ground. Grabbing her by her long ponytail, he dragged her out of our room.

"I told you to keep that anak ng demonyo away from me!" he shouted, his stinking breath in her face. "After all that he's done to me, the least he can do is leave me alone!"

"Monolith has done nothing to you!" Tita Sora cried, pushing me away as I tried to get Pa to let go of her hair.

Pa shoved me to the ground, my face scraping the floor. "That monster is the reason why my wife left me, you know. An ugly, useless, brainless child who drove her away! I just want Vera back. She doesn't answer my texts or my phone calls. But Sora, she'll talk to you, won't she? Tell my wife to come back to me now!"

"You're a monster," she said, teeth clenched. "She will never want you again."

Throwing open the front door to the super typhoon, he ripped off her glasses and threw them onto the road, the lenses shattering into tiny pieces.

"You see who isn't wanted, Sora?" he roared. He dragged her into the middle of the street, slamming her head onto the wet ground, the broken glass piercing her skin. "See how nobody wants to help you?" he asked, his voice a howl above the winds. "See how nobody cares about you? It's because you're nothing! You think you're so smart, but you're worthless!"

Tita Sora was so shocked that she couldn't even cry out.

But I knew how to make enough sound for both of us.

I fell to my knees and screamed loud enough to shake the trees.

Loud enough to turn the sky black.

Louder than the super typhoon.

Then, in the middle of the storm, as pieces of metal, wood, and tree branches flew around us, the neighbours came running.

"Tama na! Enough is enough!" they yelled, their hands filled with pots and pans, a tire iron, even a clay palayok.

They shoved Pa off of Tita Sora and hit him again and again, chasing him down the street as he slipped into the potholes and the puddles in his bare feet, struggling to get away until he disappeared into the kapeng barako fields. "Stay away from them and never come back!" they yelled, their voices a collective bellow over the screaming storm.

Tita Sora grabbed me and ran back inside, safely shutting us behind the heavy click-click door.

When she saw my wet face and the cut on my cheek, she began to cry. "I'm sorry, baby, I'm sorry," she sobbed. "I didn't know this would happen—I thought he'd changed. I never should've let him stay with us. I ignored you and I didn't keep you safe. I made a mistake. Can you ever forgive me?"

I turned her to the mirror so she would see that the bloody gashes on her own face were so much worse than mine.

Looking at my reflection, she kneeled down to my level. "From now on, you are my main priority. Lots of things are going to change soon, but everything that I'm about to do will all be for you. Promise me that no matter what happens, you'll remember that."

Pressing my nose to her cheek and breathing in the scent of rain, blood, and gravel, I gave her my promise without having to make a sound.

* * *

"Monolith, please let me in," begs the boy on the other side of my Comfort Room door. He sighs and presses his back against the wood, sliding down to the floor with a soft thump.

"Why would he open the door when he doesn't even know me?" he mutters to himself. Clearing his throat, he starts again in a cheerful tone. "Hi, I'm Jermayne. I'm from San Marco del Mudo, just like you. You can talk to me like I'm your—well, don't call me 'Kuya' or 'Ate'—just Jermayne, okay? I know you saw my clothes, so let me explain: I'm not a boy. But I'm not a girl, either. I'm trying these clothes for the first time—they're my Mumshie's. I feel good in them. Is that why you're scared of me? Look, there's nothing to be worried about. See?"

In a panic, I throw my body against the door to keep it shut, wishing there was a click-click lock. But instead of forcing the door open, Jermayne just sticks three fingers below the door, waving at my toes. The nails are painted the same ube purple as his shirt.

"Even if you don't want to talk to me and you just want to make noises, I'll still listen. Honestly, Monolith, I don't have any friends in Canada. My Mumshie's here and it's nice to be with her again, but still, it's super lonely. You understand, don't you? I know you're just five and I'm fifteen, but you and I are from the same place. Do you know how special that is? My Mumshie was even your mama's English tutor back home. Isn't that funny? San Marco isn't that big. How come we haven't met before? If you open the door for me, I'd really like to be your friend, if that's okay with you. Gusto mo bang maging kaibigan tayo?"

I hold my breath, careful not to make a sound.

The fingers wiggle again, then disappear.

* * *

I've never had a friend before.

When I was really little, Tita Sora tried to bring me to people's houses to play, but the other children were always scared of me. My hands were too strong and my head was too big and I got mad too quickly when they would ask me questions and I couldn't answer back with anything but frustrated noises.

"Talk to them," Tita Sora urged. "Come on, Monolith, try to use your words."

The kids kicked up the dust around me, playing tumbang preso and patintero, filling the sunny street with their screams and laughter, but I would just sit on the dusty curb, stacking my toy cars into a pile and then throwing them everywhere until Tita Sora gave up and decided to take me home.

"Kawawa si Sora," people always said, talking behind her back as she squatted in the gutter to collect my cars. "Parang bobo si Monolith." They pitied Tita Sora because I was so stupid.

Then, their theories would come pouring out:

"It's because his pa is an alcoholic with a bad temper."

"It's because his Lola Tering is so poor and uneducated."

"It's because his mama abandoned him to go abroad and annulled her marriage instead of trying to make it work."

There would be a chorus of tsk-tsks as they shook their heads. And then, after all that, they would settle on the one person they blamed the most:

"It's because Sora doesn't know how to parent him."

"That's true! She can't control him, so she just reads her books and lets him do whatever he wants! She's so selfish!"

"She studies like she's a doctor, but she's not even in the medical field. What a waste!"

"Sora should get married. Before long, she'll be too old to have a child of her own!"

I didn't like the way they talked about me, but I hated the way they talked about her. I started to throw tantrums every time Tita

Sora tried to get me to leave our house. Whenever she'd announce, "We're going to go out to play with your friends today!" my legs would turn to jelly, my mouth full of wails until I began to hiccup uncontrollably, only stopping when she would hold me as tightly as she could, reassuring me that we wouldn't go outside.

Eventually, she just gave up and kept us indoors, safe behind the click-click door where nobody would hurt us, and that was fine by me.

*   *   *

One night, Tita Sora said she had a surprise. Letting her hair down and putting on her best Filipiniana dress with the butterfly sleeves bigger than my head, she put me in an ironed polo shirt and black pants and dragged me out to the big town fiesta.

Everyone was curious to see me. They crowded around in their scratchy piña outfits, trying to talk to me or to tickle my neck to make me laugh, but I just looked at the ground. After being inside for so long, all of the noise and attention was too much.

"Is this the boy who doesn't speak?"

"I thought he was just a legend!"

"He's a legend, alright—at five years old, he still isn't talking!"

The strangers leaned down and jostled in front of me, thrusting their hands in my face.

"Monolith, look! Close open, close open—can you do that?"

"Clap your hands, clap your hands!"

"Beautiful eyes, beautiful eyes!"

"Where's the light?"

"High-five, Monolith! Come on, give us a high-five!"

I pushed their hands aside and groaned. I was too old for those dumb baby games. I tried to pull Tita Sora back home.

"Wait, Monolith, I want you to see the fiesta," Tita Sora said, spinning me around and leading me towards the town plaza.

"Isn't it fun? Listen to the music! Look at the lights, the food, the decorations! See the pretty banderitas swinging in the wind? And look at the parols, don't you just love the glowing stars? And over there, let's watch the dancers—see that boy and girl jumping off the highest benches for Sayaw sa Bangko? Aren't they so brave?"

I buried my face in the folds of her long, scratchy skirt and whined.

She was about to bring me towards the stage when something else captured her attention.

The church doors were open and the statue of our town's patron saint was at the front of the altar, under a warm pink spotlight from the last rays of the setting sun. People were filing out of the church for the dance performances, leaving San Marco all alone.

Tita Sora pulled me inside the church and kneeled at San Marco's shiny white feet.

"I know I'm a scientist and I haven't been to church in years, but I humbly seek your guidance and intercession," she said, her lips moving against her knuckles. "Monolith is already five years old, but he still won't speak. San Marco del Mudo, as the patron saint of mutes, you have to show me what to do. I can't keep his mother in the dark for much longer. I'm afraid that if she knows the truth, she won't want him anymore or he won't even be allowed into Canada. I need him to have a better future than the one he'll have here. You know that in this town, we don't have opportunities for children like him. I love him so much, but he deserves a better life than this. Please, San Marco, I need a miracle."

Her thin shoulders started shaking and her tears dropped onto the church floor. It made me feel sad to see her with her messy hair in her face and her special clothes getting crumpled and dirty. I took her hand from the statue and began to pull and whine. The empty church frightened me, and the only place I wanted to be was back behind the click-click door where we would both be safe.

"Monolith, what will I do with you?" Tita Sora asked, her voice strained.

While the fiesta went on behind us, she let me pull her back home.

As Tita Sora helped me get ready for bed, she touched her forehead to mine. "I think I know how to help you. Things are going to change soon, but remember—everything is all for you."

Then, she pulled me into my favourite hug of all: the one that was so tight that I couldn't move my arms because all I could feel was her love around me and nothing else.

*   *   *

After she talked to San Marco del Mudo in the church, Tita Sora gave me a thin metal object. I thought it was for drawing, so I pressed a crayon to it and she laughed.

"No Monolith, this isn't paper. It's an iPad. We used up lots and lots and lots of your mama's remittance money to buy it, so be careful, okay? Look, I already loaded it with three English shows. You can watch *Peppa Pig*, *Bubble Guppies*, and *Paw Patrol*. Isn't that fun?"

The English names sounded like funny noises to me, but when she pressed her finger to the screen and it lit up with brightly coloured videos of characters singing and dancing and playing games, I couldn't stop watching. It was like looking at a happier place where there were people who were always excited to see me.

But then one day, Tita Sora woke me up to tell me that she was leaving me.

"I have to take my exams in Los Baños," she said. "I'm so close to graduating and getting the research fellowship that I want, so I really need to focus. I'll be back in two weeks. You'll stay with your Lola Tering, okay?"

I whimpered but she knelt down to meet me eye-to-eye. "Monolith, what did you promise me? Remember that everything I'm doing is for you." I gulped and nodded.

Lola Tering had a tiny farmer's shack where the shows on my iPad never worked. I dragged my feet the entire way.

But to my surprise, Tita Sora walked right past the shack and stopped in front of the most beautiful house I'd ever seen: an old bahay na bato of wood and stone, with windowpanes made of capiz shells that glowed a bright white in the sun. My mouth dropped open. It looked like something out of a dream.

Lola Tering came outside to greet us, her old eyes crinkling into a smile.

Peering up at the crumbling walls, Tita Sora asked, "Are you sure this old house has internet? Monolith needs to watch his shows so he can learn English."

"Don't worry, I'll put him in the big room closest to the router," she said. "He'll even have a new friend waiting for him there."

Tita Sora hugged her goodbye, planting a kiss on her wrinkled cheek. "You're the best, Nanay."

As Tita Sora rushed away to catch the bus to Los Baños, I started shrieking for her to come back, but Lola Tering swiftly interrupted my tantrum with a gift.

"Look, my darling apo, I got you a new backpack," she said. She pointed at the scary monster with the open mouth frozen in mid-scream. "See, that's you—the Incredible Hulk!"

I scrunched my mouth as tightly as I could. I wasn't green and ugly like that monster. I was about to throw myself into the dirt in protest when she unzipped my backpack and put my precious iPad inside. When she slung the backpack onto my shoulders, she stopped in front of a window and had me look at my reflection. "See how grown-up you look! What a big boy! So smart!"

No one except Tita Sora had ever called me "smart" before. I stood up straighter, pulling the backpack straps tighter on my shoulders. My head held high, I followed her into the house.

Lola Tering brought me up the stairs to a large, dim room. Even though the curtains were closed, the air wasn't too hot because there were multiple fans pointed at a big wooden bed piled high with lots of soft pillows. And in the bed, there was a thin old man with wrinkled, greyish skin who stared curiously at me. I went behind the door, looking for a click-click lock.

"My caregiving job just got even easier," Lola Tering said, pulling me toward the foot of the bed. "You don't talk, Lolo Bayani doesn't talk, and you can both keep each other company. It's perfect!" Reaching into my backpack, she said, "Here's your iPad, Monolith. Show Lolo Bayani how it works. Keep each other company while I go to the market, okay?" Shutting the door behind her, she left us alone.

Lolo Bayani was a stranger, but he didn't look like he could hurt me. He held out his hand for me to make mano, but I was too busy to do that. I poked his old feet, his bony hip, his thin arm, his wrinkled cheek. When he didn't react and just focused his big, curious eyes on mine, I relaxed. I pulled out my iPad and snuggled up next to him. We had just met, but it was like I knew him already. I felt very safe, even without the click-click door.

I could have stayed there forever.

I wish I did.

* * *

On the floor of the locked Comfort Room in Toronto, I curl up onto the bath mat and fall asleep.

And when I wake up, I'm back in San Marco, in that big bahay na bato, waking up in Lolo Bayani's bed.

"Gising na, Monolith," a deep male voice sings out. "Wake up, I have something to tell you!"

I roll over, my arm reaching out for Lolo Bayani beside me, but he's not there. Blinking my eyes open, I don't see the usual darkness of his room, but instead, every corner is glowing with long candles. I peek beneath the bed, into the aparador, and out of the window, but I don't see him anywhere.

"Monolith," the voice calls out, "when your Tita Sora left you in Canada, she was so heartbroken that she accidentally took your iPad back to San Marco with her. She gave it to me so I could see all of my messages from my children and grandchildren in Canada. I don't need it anymore. Parine ka! Come here if you want it back!"

Curious, I leave the bedroom and follow the voice to the sala, where I find Lolo Bayani at the piano, leafing through a yellowed music book with my old iPad tucked snugly under his arm. He stands tall in a bright white barong Tagalog. His face isn't thin and grey anymore, and his voice is deep and strong. He offers me the iPad, but I shake my head, pushing it away, unable to take my eyes off of him.

A smile spreads across his face. "No more iPad, eh?" He offers me his hand, and I know what to do.

I lean forward and slowly take his hand in mine, pressing his fingers against my forehead. It has been so long since I've made mano. We both grin at each other.

"I'm so glad that you got the invitation to my party," he says. "I've been wanting you to experience this for so long. Now say 'Salamat po'—can you do that for me?"

I shake my head slowly, the words frozen in my throat.

He crouches down to me, his healthy, glowing face at level with mine. "Now Monolith, I'm not saying you shouldn't learn English, but before that language invades your mind, I need you to feel the language of your heart," he says. "Tagalog contains the music of the land where generations upon generations of your ancestors have lived. Once you have the language inside of you, no matter how far you go or how long you're away, the words will always help you find your way back home."

He spreads his arm wide, and the house transforms behind him. Once filled with scratchy old furniture covered in dust and cobwebs, the sala is now shiny and warm, with polished wooden arches, a gleaming floor, and capiz-shell lights that glow in every corner. As the room fills up with dozens of women wearing long, butterfly-sleeve dresses and men wearing crisp white barongs, they sway with the music as Lolo Bayani sings,

Pilipinas kong minumutya	*Philippines, my beloved*
Pugad ng luha ko at dalita	*Nest of tears and suffering*
Aking adhika	*My wish for you*
Makita kang	*Is to see you*
Sakdal laya!	*Completely free!*

His deep voice is bigger than any typhoon. I can feel his song echoing through the town plaza, off Mount Batulao and across the Tagaytay Ridge, riding the waves of the rivers and oceans, and bringing tears to the eyes of every Filipino around the world, making them all turn in the direction of San Marco del Mudo. As his audience bursts into enthusiastic applause, Lolo Bayani takes a deep bow.

"Ladies and gentlemen, that kundiman, 'Bayan Ko,' is for my dear friend Monolith, who, during some of my darkest days, stayed beside me and gave me a reason to live. Because of him, I reunited with my family, and because of him, tonight, I am able to leave this earth as a happy man. It is my final wish that even in Canada, Monolith will never forget the beauty of Tagalog—that our proud words will live inside of him forever!"

The audience applauds again, everyone turning to smile at me.

Walking through the crowd, Lolo Bayani meets me beneath the shiny wooden arches and I bury myself deep into his strong arms.

"Did you like my kundiman?" he asks.

I nod, whining into his chest.

"Use your words, Monolith. I'm listening." He bends down low and taps his ear. "I sang a song for you, so what do you say? If you enjoyed it, you can say thank you. Try it for me now: salamat po."

"Salamat po," I whisper shyly. I thank him so quietly that I can barely hear myself.

"Say it again," he says. "No one will hurt you for being loud. No one will love you less. No one will abandon you. I want to hear what you have to say. Say it again." He smiles so brightly that I touch his face and see that where my hand presses against his cheek, there is a capiz-shell glow that spreads throughout my entire body.

I wrap my arms around his neck and repeat myself again and again, my voice getting louder with each word. "Salamat, salamat, salamat po!"

* * *

I wake up to the sound of Jermayne talking to someone. The magic and warmth of Lolo Bayani's sala is gone, and I'm back on the orange bath mat again. I strain to hear kundiman, but I can only hear Jermayne's nervous voice. I slowly crack open the door to peek at him sitting on the floor in the dark, the phone lighting up his worried face.

"Pa, it's me. No, I'm not with Mumshie right now. I'm staying with a friend for the next week. We're going to take care of each other. It'll be fine. But since I'm alone right now, I wanted to call. I've been meaning to talk to you about something important."

"Okay, what is it? You want to come home?"

"No, not that."

"You want me to come there? Because Jermayne—"

"No, no. I want to talk to you about something else, Pa." Jermayne takes a deep breath, holding the phone with shaking hands. "I want you to know that I decided I'm not going to be called 'he' anymore. That isn't my preferred pronoun."

"Preferred pronoun? Ano?" The faraway voice pauses for a minute. "So you'll be a girl now?"

"No, Pa. I'm not a boy, and I'm not a girl. I'm in an in-between space. I've decided that I'm going to be using they/them pronouns from now on."

"They/them," the man repeats slowly.

"Honestly, I wish English had a singular gender-neutral pronoun like 'siya' in Tagalog," Jermayne says, their words spilling out faster and faster. "But then I was thinking, this really shouldn't be a big deal. I mean, you know how in Tagalog, it's not 'son' or 'daughter'; it's just 'anak'—child? And how it's not 'brother' or 'sister'; it's just 'kapatid'—sibling? It was the Spanish colonizers who made us change to fit their ideas of gender! It isn't even true to our original Filipino culture. So me being non-binary and using they/them pronouns from now on shouldn't be a big deal, right? I'm just being more of the person I'm supposed to be. Please don't be mad. I've been wanting to tell you this for a long time and I just didn't know how to do it until now but I—"

The man clears his throat.

Jermayne holds their breath and so do I.

"I just put up a new exhibit at the museum," the man says. "Your Tita Marki helped me design it."

Jermayne groans. "I finally tell you this and you just want to talk about work?"

"It's about the babaylan and katalonan, with a very special display about the asog and bayog."

"So you have an exhibit about the pre-colonial leaders? Great."

"They shaped Philippine history with their influence by defending the weak, warding off evil, and sharing their healing knowledge. The babaylan and katalonan were instrumental in creating a better society for everyone. People often think they were all women, but this isn't true. The asog and bayog were a special kind of healer from what you just called 'the in-between space.' They were extraordinary in so many ways, and they helped form Philippine society to make it better for everyone." The man clears his throat again, his voice cracking this time. "Jermayne, this exhibit isn't just inspired by Philippine history—it's inspired by you."

Jermayne gasps. "Pa, you didn't."

"I've known you were different for some time now, and I shouldn't have pushed you away. It's just that the closer we got to our travel date, it became clearer that you would have to leave for Canada without me. I realized that I could never leave San Marco, but I knew this wasn't where you belonged. I told myself that you would be fine on your own, and that I just would've held you back. I'm sorry I wasn't truthful to you. You wouldn't believe how much I've missed you."

"You really hurt me."

"I know, and I'm so sorry. I was a coward. I let you and your Mumshie down. And now, I'm missing the chance to watch you grow up."

Jermayne's tears fall all over the screen.

"Every day, I think about how brave you were, making that long journey alone. I wouldn't have been able to do that at fifteen years old—let alone nowadays, at my age! And now, look at you, calling to tell me who you are. So self-assured, so smart—you're more than I will ever be. I'm so proud of you."

"You are?"

"I always will be. But can you forgive me for not being there with you?"

"You know what, I can," they reply, sniffling. "You're already in the place where you belong. I understand that."

"I love you so much, Jermayne."

"I love you too, Pa." Jermayne wipes their eyes. "Hey, will you send me pictures of the museum exhibit?"

"Absolutely. But if something's missing, you tell me, okay?"

"I will."

Turning off the phone, Jermayne sits for a few minutes, smiling as they wipe their tears away.

Then, they notice me standing in the open door.

"Monolith, you're awake! Did you hear me talking?"

I nod and step closer.

Jermayne looks at me cautiously. "Are you finally ready to be friends with me?"

I nod again.

"Did you understand what I said? That I'm not a boy or a girl—I'm in between? Is that okay? Can we still be friends?"

I bounce on my heels, nodding the whole time. But before I can say a word, my stomach growls loudly and they burst out laughing.

"Okay, okay. Now that we're friends, want to help me figure out what to make for dinner?"

* * *

Jermayne doesn't know how to cook anything. They can't figure out how to turn on Mama's rice cooker. They burn the pandesal in the toaster. They try to open some Spam, but when they break off the tiny metal key, they don't know how to open the can without it. They try slamming it on the counter and smashing it beneath their winter boots, but nothing works.

"The good news is that I have a whole week to figure this out," they say, smiling guiltily. "Aren't you glad your mama left you with me?"

My stomach growls again as I wrinkle my nose.

Jermayne rummages through the cupboards and finds a big box of Hello Panda and two bright blue cans of Gina. As we feast on a dinner of chocolate-filled cookies and mango juice, they mimic everything I do.

When I smash a cookie into my mouth, so do they.

When I blow bubbles into my juice, so do they.

When I make my happy squealing noises, so do they.

And best of all, when I laugh, they laugh even harder.

Soon, we race around the apartment, leaving our cookie-crumb handprints on every single wall, shouting at the top of our lungs. We bang Singkil rhythms on the glass windows and we wrap ourselves in long curtain dresses and we throw toy cars at the angry green face on my Incredible Hulk backpack and we run around in circles, spinning round and round like a super typhoon until finally, we collapse in the upside-down apartment, tired but happy.

Jermayne lies on the floor beside my mattress. We both look up at the ceiling, catching our breath.

"This is fun, but I can't help but think that it's kind of sad that our mamas are with their employers right now," they say. "I mean, this is our first March Break in Canada, and they just abandoned us to go take care of those Canadian families. Our mothers left us for other families before, but it hurts to be left behind again when we're finally here, right?" Jermayne puts their hands under their head. "And you know what else doesn't make any sense? Back home, my dance teacher always said that we were performing to represent the motherland, but that always bothered me. So many of us didn't even have our mamas in the audience. I always wondered, why is it called 'the motherland' when it isn't even where our mothers are?"

I throw another toy car at the face of the Incredible Hulk.

"Were you ever mad that you were left behind?"

I shrug. I was just a baby when Mama left, so I didn't even miss her. The only time when I really felt left behind was when Tita Sora brought me to Canada.

She said we were going on a special adventure, and she gave me some medicine to make me ready. Hours later, when I woke up in the airplane, I was so scared that I began clawing at my seat-belt, wanting to take it off. But when Tita Sora tried to loosen it for me, I scratched her arms, leaving big, angry red marks across her skin. I tried to tell her I was sorry, but she whispered something to a worried lady who was wearing a dress with a plane pin. They gave me some more medicine to make me relax. After that, I only remember pieces: a cold white room, a serious yellow-haired lady looking at some papers, a car ride with Tita Sora's whispering friends, the warm feeling of her nose pressing against my cheek.

And then, when I woke up in the morning, she had disappeared. The person I loved the most in the whole world was gone, and in her place was a stranger who kept talking to me in English and calling me "Monobaby" like she knew me.

I did what I needed to do. I destroyed her apartment, trying to figure out where Tita Sora could be hiding. I punched and slapped and kicked the lady, trying to figure out why she was calling herself "Mama" when she was just a stranger to me. As I hurt her again and again, I wanted to scream, "If you're really my mama, where were you when everyone said that I was stupid? Where were you when Tita Sora cried at the feet of San Marco because I couldn't talk? Where were you when Pa got mad and hurt her in the street because of me? What kind of mama wouldn't be there for all of those things?"

But since I didn't have the words, my hands had to talk for me. I hit her over and over to say no to the strange words coming out of her mouth, no to her insisting that I become "Doctor Monolith," no to her being my mother, no to being in Canada, no to this entire new life that I didn't want.

But then Mama's friends, Miss Magda and Mister Jan, started coming over to tie me up at bedtime. They made her take me to that children's centre where Mama let Miss Forte film me even when all I wanted to do was scream. I thought it would be better when Mama and I moved to Toronto and she left me with Kuya Paulo, who was a Filipino, too. But when he tried to make me listen to him read his English book, I got angry and I told him no with my hands. Mama let him give me medicine that made me feel just like I did in the airplane—too sleepy to do anything.

But whenever I was back in the studio apartment and his medicine wore off, I couldn't stop screaming, even late into the night, because my entire world had turned upside down and that was the only sound my heart wanted to make.

*   *   *

After the sun goes down, Jermayne doesn't turn the lights on. Instead, they lie beside me on the floor. Turning on a flashlight, they draw zigzags of soft white light across the ceiling. It makes me feel calm to watch the patterns forming over and over in the dark. And after awhile, I realize that it's not a zigzag, but it's one letter over and over: M, M, M.

"Hey Monolith, do you know what your name means?" Jermayne asks. "It's an English word for a giant stone. If something's a monolith, that means that you look at it and you see exactly what it is. Like the cliffs of San Marco del Mudo—those are a monolith, because they're big pieces of straight rock, nothing more. But honestly, I don't think you're like that. There's a lot more to you than people see. Do you know what I mean?"

They hold their hand up in the air and I give them a high-five.

As we lie in the upside-down apartment, I copy their breathing, feeling my chest rising and falling with theirs. I feel good for the first time in a long, long time. Not totally happy, but not totally sad, either.

I feel in-between with Jermayne, and that's better than I've felt in a long time.

Suddenly, there's a knock at the door.

I start thinking about all of the people it could be, and Jermayne sees me sit up straight, my eyes big and my mouth frozen in an *O*.

"Monolith! What's wrong?"

I hiss at them, trying to make them whisper.

The knocks get louder and more insistent. They sound like the knocks from Pa when he came to our house smelling like alcohol and rain. If it's not Pa, it's Miss Magda and Mister Jan with the hugging jacket. Or it's Miss Forte with her camera. Or it's Kuya Paulo with his sleepytime pills. I want to tell Jermayne to leave the door shut and hide with me, but the words are stuck in my throat.

"I'm going to see who it is," Jermayne says, putting on a brave smile. "They didn't buzz into the building, so maybe it's one of your neighbours. Maybe your mama sent someone to check on us."

I want to wail but I'm too scared to make a sound, so I dart behind the curtains and hide. My feelings must be contagious because just as Jermayne reaches the door, they pull Mama's soft grass walis tambo from the closet, gripping it upside-down so the handle is like a blunt sword.

I bite the curtains so that I don't scream.

Jermayne opens the door just slightly, the walis in their shaky hand.

"Hello," a woman says in English. "Is Monolith here?"

I peek out from behind the curtain.

Immediately, I launch myself over our mess and push Jermayne aside to throw the door open.

Standing there with two big suitcases, her glasses all fogged up and her long ponytail covered in fresh March snow, is the person I love the most in the whole entire world.

"My baby!" she cries, falling backwards into the hallway as I fling myself straight into her arms. "You got so big! Ohh, I missed you!"

"Who are you?" Jermayne asks, suspicious.

"I just arrived from San Marco del Mudo. Ate Vera said you'd be here. Nice to meet you, Jermayne!"

Their eyes narrow into tiny slits. "How long are you staying? Are you here for March Break?"

"I was accepted for a special environmental research fellowship at the University of Toronto," she replies. "I'll be here for six months. Maybe even longer if everything goes well and they accept my international student application. I know you weren't expecting me, but I wanted to keep it a secret in case it didn't work out. I didn't want Monolith to be disappointed."

"Well, I'm babysitting Monolith right now," Jermayne says, protectively pulling me off of her and out of the hallway. "He's my responsibility all week."

Tita Sora peeks into the apartment and turns on the light, taking in my toys scattered all over the floor, the lopsided curtains, the dining table covered in smashed cookies and sticky mango juice, and the chocolate fingerprints all over the walls and windows. "Well, the place looks perfect," she says, her mouth twitching into a smile.

Jermayne blocks her from coming inside. "Again, who are you?"

She smiles. "That's right, I didn't introduce myself properly. I'm Monolith's—"

"Nanay Sora!" I yell.

She always called herself my Tita Sora, but my heart knows that I'm not going to call her this out loud. She's not my mama, but she's not my tita, either. She is more than that: she is the Tagalog word for mother.

"Nanay Sora!" I holler again, the words filling the air like Lolo Bayani's big voice as he sang his favourite kundiman.

Jermayne's jaw drops. "He can talk?"

"Monolith! You can talk!" she cries, scooping me up and squeezing me so tight, just the way that I like it. Holding me in her arms, she spins around and around the apartment and all I can focus on is her huge smile.

When she gets out of breath, she sets me down. "But wait, Monolith, you're wrong. You can't call me 'Nanay'—I'm your aunt, not your mother. You have to call me *Tita* Sora."

I hop from foot to foot, grinning. "Nanay Sora! Nanay Sora!"

"I think he just gave you a new title," Jermayne says.

She kneels down, putting her hands on my shoulders. "Are you sure? Monolith, I can't believe that you want to call me 'Nanay' after everything I've done to you," she says, her eyes filling with tears. "How could you ever forgive me?"

I touch her cheek, noticing that the scars from Pa are faint, but still there.

"When I had to leave you here, I went back to the airport so fast. I didn't want to get in the way of you and your mama, and I thought it would be easier for all of us if I just left you with her."

Jermayne crosses their arms and huffs.

"I thought I was doing the right thing, but then your mama kept sending me messages about how hard it was for you. She said you were angry all of the time and I knew that wasn't who you are. I worked so hard to get this fellowship so that I could come back to Canada to be with you. I'm sorry it took so long. I've missed you every single day. Monolith, can you ever forgive me?"

I press my cheek against hers. "Nanay Sora," I say, the words easily falling out of my mouth as if I've said them a million times out loud, instead of just in my mind.

She puts her hand on my cheek and laughs, her eyes filled with joy and relief.

I'm so happy that I want to scream and scream and scream, but instead, I pull Jermayne and Nanay Sora close, as tightly as I can, and I feel like my entire world is new again.

I'm finally home.

Acknowledgements

I AM SO FORTUNATE that this book has been supported by an entire community.

My husband JC—I still can't believe that you put in our wedding invitations that I'd write two books someday. You never flinched during the lean times, you made me an honorary Bonifacio, you kept Cheeseburger happy whenever I fell into a writing hole, and you braved the Quiapo crowds so we could touch the sole of the Black Nazarene on Christmas Day. Now that the book is out, you can finally say, "You did it!"

My sister Jamela—you paved the way for me in countless ways. Thank you for being such a superstar English student that I will forever consider you to be the first Filipino-Canadian writer I have ever met.

My mom Jasmin—every week, you took me on the one-hour bus rides to the Sarnia Public Library so I could go to storytime, but still, you wondered how I became a writer! I'm so grateful that you gave me kundiman piano music; Chapter 7 wouldn't have been written without it. Thank you for being so proud of me—and for making your BHS and PNC batchmates proud of me, too.

My dad—for giving me the childhood that you never had and for making so many of my dreams possible, I'll always be grateful.

To my extended family (Perez, Bonifacio, and beyond!), thank you for the inspiration and support. We may not have a nurse in the family, but at least we have a writer. Charot!

My childhood friend, Jennifer Hau—Whenever something good happens to me, I will forever celebrate by texting you, "LOOK WHAT YOU DID!!!" Thank you for being the one to push me off a cliff and into the literary world.

My Pluma family—I'm so grateful that our collective of Fil-Can writers exists; I've found my people in all of you. Shout-out to Nastasha Alli and Gelaine Santiago for encouraging me to explore my hometown in Chapter 6, to Shirley Camia for consulting about Iqaluit life in Chapter 3, and to Shirley and Jaisa Sulit for being the literary midwives who helped me get Chapter 2 into the world in under a week! Special thanks goes to Eric Tigley for his lessons in Philippine history and to Motzie Dapul for providing her Filipino expertise through her Tagalog review.

The Filipino-Canadian Writers and Journalists Network— you always believed that I would get published someday, and you celebrated with me every step of the way. Special thanks to Mila and Hermie Garcia at *The Philippine Reporter* for seeing a journalist in me.

My fellow Little Manila tour guides—thanks to Diana Roldan and Ysh Cabaña for always shining a light on Little Manila with me. More Little Manila stories to come, always.

The Banff Centre for Arts and Culture—thank you for the Masters funding so that I could attend the Emerging Writers Intensive and meet my First Chapter Novel group! Much appreciation to Betty Ann Adam, Hali Heavy Shield, and Rhonda Gladue for the feedback with Chapters 1 and 4, and special shout-outs to Jan Guenther Braun for helping me capture the marital spat in

Chapter 5, to Omar Ramirez for bringing the bahay na bato to life in Chapter 7, to K.R. Byggdin for Jermayne's non-binary coming-of-age moments in Chapter 8, and to Sam K. MacKinnon who told me that if I was at the point when I couldn't bear to look at something anymore, it was time to send it off into the world. (For the emerging authors out there, take Sam's advice!)

The Slow Writers Club—For a writer juggling multiple jobs, having a group with regular writing times is so valuable. I'm especially grateful to Sharon Bala and Melanie Mah who pushed me to submit to agents long after I thought it was possible, and who encouraged me to write the longest acknowledgements ever.

The Asian-Canadian Writers Workshop—it was an honour for this book to be a finalist for the Jim Wong-Chu Emerging Writers Award. Special thanks to Ted Alcuitas for putting this opportunity on my radar; it was the push I needed.

My literary Ate, Catherine Hernandez—I've been so grateful to receive your advice and encouragement, and I'm honoured that you were the first author to blurb this book. Thank you for being a bright light for so many of us across the diaspora.

My mentors—thank you Joshua Whitehead, for seeing potential from the first line of this book and inviting me to the Banff Centre, and to Richard Scarsbrook, for the early encouragement at Humber. Special thanks to the women who provided me with beautiful blurbs: to Kim Echlin for spotting something special in my work years ago, when I needed it most, and to Kyo Maclear, for inspiring me to let Monolith shine in Chapter 9. And I'm especially grateful to Wayson Choy, who told me that one day, we would be colleagues. Wayson, you are missed, but your faith in me lives on.

And of course, to Karen Connelly—I'll always remember how I introduced myself to you at the Humber School for Writers by blurting out that I'd just left settlement work and that I felt like I was bleeding stories. When you laughed and assured me that you would help me triage, I knew I was in good hands! Thank you for introducing me to Westwood Creative Artists.

My agents—I'm so fortunate to have not one, but *two* sounding boards in Bridgette Kam and Hilary McMahon at WCA! Four years after we first connected, you welcomed this completely unexpected book and changed the course of my life. It means so much to have you in my corner.

My team at Douglas & McIntyre—Thank you to Anna Comfort O'Keeffe for the quick and wholehearted response to these stories, and to Corina Eberle, Annie Boyar, and Luke Inglis for their marketing expertise. I'm especially grateful to Caroline Skelton, Anya Naval, Emma Biron, and Artie Goshulak for their incredibly insightful editing and their shared love of this kaleidoscope of characters.

To Christine Mangosing—you designed the marketing material for so many community events that shaped how I learned about Filipino identity, history, and culture. It was an honour to have you design for me!

To France Stohner, Estela Aguilar, and the social workers who generously shared their feedback with me—your insights on Iqaluit, Côte-des-Neiges, and Monolith's care were so appreciated. And thank you to Janice Sapigao for being the first person to prove that my Canadian stories could cross borders. Just like it was an honour to be in TAYO, it's an honour to have you blurb my book. Thank you for embodying the meaning of kapwa.

My 1200+ Filipino Talks students—I'm forever proud to say that I'm the youngest in my family, but an Ate to many. Three of these stories are from teen voices because so much of this book is inspired by you. I hope you find yourselves in these pages.

My Filipino Talks educators and settlement workers—everything I've ever talked about is in this book: remittances, cultural shame, separation and reunification, utang na loob, and so much more. May this book inspire the discussions in your classrooms and community workshops that you've been wanting to have.

To the team behind the documentary *When Strangers Re-unite*—when I was an undergraduate student, your documentary was my first opportunity to see Filipino caregivers onscreen. Thank you for inspiring the title of this book.

The Katimavik program—experiencing this nine-month service-learning adventure changed the way that I saw our vast country. Thank you for the opportunity to see Canada so that years later, I could write about it.

My colleagues over the past twenty years in the settlement sector—you encouraged me to approach this work with creativity, and I cannot thank you enough for this support. Special thanks goes to Maria Guiao for her unbelievable power of inspiration, to Marina Zybina who pushed me to start my Filipino Talks journey in the TDSB, and to my Together Project team for giving me the support I needed to pursue my dreams.

To Dr. Philip Kelly, Dr. Don Wells, and Carmen Condo of the HCDSB Pinoy Project—working with you showed me the power of community-based research in schools. Thank you for seeing something special in me and for putting me on a microphone time and time again.

The Toronto Arts Council, the Ontario Arts Council, and the Canada Council for the Arts—your grants showed me that I was doing something important and necessary. May you forever help emerging authors see their potential.

To Kapisanan Philippine Centre for Arts and Culture—salamuch for the incredible events, the artistic magic, the Tagalog classes, the history lessons, and the wonderful community you have fostered over the years.

To the great kundiman masters whose work is featured in Chapter 7—it is my sincerest hope that your songs live on forever: "Kundiman (Anak-Dalita)" by Francisco Santiago, text by Deogracias A. Rosario; "Pakiusap" by Francisco Santiago, text by José Corazón de Jesús; "Minamahal Kita" by Dominador Santiago, text by Mike Velarde; "Ikaw Rin!" music and text by Nicanor Abelardo; "Pahimakas" by Nicanor Abelardo, text José Corazón de Jesús; "Dahil Sa Iyo" by Miguel Velarde Jr., text by Dominador Santiago; "Madaling Araw" by José Corazón de Jesús, text by Francisco Santiago; "Nasaan Ka Irog?" by Nicanor Abelardo, text by José Corazón de Jesús; "Himutok" by Nicanor Abelardo; "Hindi Kita Malimot" by Josefino Cenizal, and "Bayan Ko" by Constancio De Guzman, text by José Corazón de Jesús. Special thank you to Dr. Quiliano Niñeza Anderson for his PhD research on kundiman, and Likhawit Enterprises for their *Kundiman Atbp Piano Selections* songbook.

Lastly, thank you to the many Filipino associations dedicated to connecting our diaspora across generations. When I was a gawky teenager learning pandanggo sa Ilaw in Sarnia, I never could've imagined that one day, I'd write a whole book about our community. Your impact is immeasurable.

Salamat po sa inyong lahat!